IN LOVE WITH A DARK STRANGER

IMARI JADE

First Printing: 2010

ISBN: 978-1-68046-544-0

Melange Books, LLC
White Bear Lake, MN 55110
www.melange-books.com

Published in the United States of America.

Cover Design by Caroline Andrus

CHAPTER 1

"Stop them," someone shouted in broken English.

Bethany looked up just in time to see four men on horseback headed her way. Thinking quickly, she jumped backwards, upsetting a cartload of perfume, and narrowly escaping a group of children as they scurried out of the way. The first two horses, two magnificent beasts neared. Their riders were masked, making identification impossible. She, on the other hand, stood out like a sore thumb in her dark American made pantsuit, sunglasses, and a straw hat. Had it not been for the fact that she needed appropriate climate-friendly clothes, she wouldn't be caught dead outside in such an outfit. She got up, apologizing to the vendor, just as the two horses approached. The rider on the first horse looked down on her as they rode by. For one fleeting moment, their eyes locked. He winked and then rode off with the other man, leaving behind a mob of angry shoppers, venders and two very slow police officers who gave up the chase.

"Damn bandits," one of them said as he dismounted and came to her rescue. "Are you injured?" Their uniforms were a khaki colored tunic, pants, and cap. He lowered his gun and put it back in the belt holster. Like most of the men there, he wore a stylish beard and goatee.

"I'm fine," she assured him, even though she didn't know how much English he knew. Her Arabic was horrible.

"We are sorry for your inconvenience."

His English was passable. "Thank you. Who were those men?"

"Common criminals. We have been chasing them for some time now. They rob the tombs of their treasures and sell them for profit."

Bethany frowned. "Outrageous. I hope you catch them soon. I came all the way to Egypt to see those treasures they are pilfering."

"Are you here on vacation?"

"No. I'm an archeologist. I'm here to participate in a dig near the Valley of the Kings."

He smiled. "Welcome to Cairo. I hope you don't let this incident spoil your visit."

"Thank you, and no, it won't."

The other officer called to him. He bowed and mounted his horse. "Have a pleasant stay."

Bethany bowed respectfully. "I will." The two officers rode off, leaving her a bit perplexed about how to make restitution to the perfume vendor.

"It's okay," the woman said to her. "Nothing is broken."

"Thank you. I'm not usually so clumsy."

She smiled and waved Bethany on. "A wink from Al-Shar Khan would make me clumsy too."

"Who is Al-Shar Khan?"

The woman fanned herself with her hand. "Al-Shar Khan is that big strapping fellow that almost ran you over, whose kisses are so passionate that they'll sweep you off your feet."

Bethany smirked. The woman sounded like she had firsthand knowledge of the cur, which Bethany doubted since the woman was probably old enough to be her mother. "Thank you," she said after finally making a purchase. She waved goodbye and walked through the crowded streets of Wekala-Al-Balqa. There were people everywhere hawking their goods in a language completely foreign to her. She had only been in town a couple of days but she had fallen in love with the historical place. Like the United States, Egypt was a mix of cultures…Egyptians, Muslims, Berbers, Bedouins, Nubians, and an American here and there.

Talk about tourist attractions. They were everywhere from the pyramids to the desert. She was only supposed to be there a couple of months and would not get a chance to see it all. But if it was up to her she would never leave. "Kisses that would knock me off my feet," she repeated as she sat down for a cool drink at a local café. The thought nearly made her swoon. To be kissed senseless by a man was what she'd always desired, but unfortunately, she never found anyone who cared enough to make her feel special. And Mark was the worst. Funny, it had been five months and the hurt was still deep. This trip to Egypt was meant to put him out of her mind forever. So, she planned to bury herself in her work until he was just a memory. Suddenly feeling cool from the fruity orange drink, Bethany rose, grabbed her packages and decided to call an end to her shopping excursion. She had too many packages to walk back to the hotel with, so she did the next best thing…she hailed a taxi.

"Whew, that was close," Jamaal Wadud Hatem said as he hopped off his horse. "Did we have to go through the bazaar? We could have run someone over."

Al-Shar Khan dismounted and led his Arabian horse into a stall. "It couldn't be helped. The police were on our asses like we're a bunch of criminals."

"Technically we were in an unauthorized cemetery." Jamaal stabled his caramel colored horse in a stall next to Al-Shar's deep chocolate colored stallion.

"We weren't looting it." He closed the stall and waited for Jamaal to join him.

"They think we were. In fact, it's now common knowledge that they are looking for us."

"Hence the disguises," Al-Shar said as he opened a door and walked down the stairs that led to a hidden passageway below the ground. He lit a lantern and Jamaal followed him down, securing the door behind them. It was getting harder and harder for them to get to those in need. Like thieves in the night he and Jamaal searched the cemeteries looking for the poor and homeless and provided them with food and necessities of life. When not involved in humanitarian duties, they hunted the tombs for looters.

Then there were the times when they had to meet with some unscrupulous characters to get much needed information. Today had been such an occasion. One of their paid informants had knowledge of two looters who were looking to trade some goods with him. This exchange of goods would cost a very high price, should he accept…even though it meant losing ten of his finest Arabian horses.

They came to the end of the tunnel. Al-Shar turned off the lantern and opened the door. Jamaal brought up the rear. They stepped inside a room brilliant with light.

"I better get going," Jamaal replied with a yawn. "I'm tired and need something cold to drink."

Al-Shar nodded. "We'll meet back here at sunset."

Jamaal left through another door, leaving him alone to think. He removed the keffiyeh from his head and thick black curly hair cascaded down his shoulders. He removed his fake beard and scratched at his own scraggly beard and mustache. "I need a shave and a bath before going to see the folks." He removed the burnoose from around his shoulders, dropped it in the hamper, and headed toward his bedroom. Once there he removed the wig and took the dark contacts from his eyes.

He removed his tunic and stepped beneath the hot shower spray, turning around to let the drops massage his aching shoulders, back and behind. Make no mistake he loved horses but they weren't the most comfortable ride in the world. Images of the American woman from the bazaar entered his mind as he rubbed the soap across his chest.

Al closed his eyes, conjuring up those blue eyes and coral-colored lips. He had been with many women since he reached puberty, but never an American. They were taboo, things to be watched and feared. *Then why am I suddenly hardening in the nether regions?*

He moved his hand down and soaped up his pubic area. His penis pointed upward toward his navel. *Damn this overactive libido.* Their eyes had only met for a moment but it was enough to spark an interest in him even though he knew that their paths would never cross again.

He gripped his phallus in his free palm and slowly began to massage it. Unlike most men he was not ashamed to masturbate. He had discovered girls at an early age, but had been taught to respect them. But that did nothing for that achy feeling he experienced whenever around them. His virginity was taken by one of the women in his godfather's harem and from there he never looked back. He found comfort and solitude in the arms of one woman after another since then. He sighed. But lately all he felt was emptiness after the act was over. Maybe there was such a thing as too much sex. He pressed his hand to the side of the shower stall and braced himself as he came.

"Ah," he gasped as his body shuddered and released the rapid flow of semen. Looking down he watched as it swirled in the water and seeped down the drain. "What a waste."

CHAPTER 2

$\mathcal{B}$ethany paid the taxi driver and then carried her bags inside the lobby of the hotel where she was temporarily living. She struggled past the small reception desk and continued over to the elevator, which she took up to her room on the fifth floor. By some miracle, she found her key card amongst her packages and cluttered purse, and nearly passed out from heat exhaustion once she made it inside. A cool blast from the air conditioning unit revived her enough to put away her purchases.

Except for being run over by a bunch of horses her morning turned out to be very nice. After a quick shower and a change of clothes, she felt refreshed and ready to take on the fellows. She found them in the hotel business room taking up most of the tables with maps and coffee cups.

George Eisemann her ex-archeology professor and current boss had removed his jacket and rolled up his shirtsleeves. George was her father's friend. He was a very nice man with soulful brown eyes, and a beard and mustache that reminded her of Santa Claus, except the color was more mingled gray than white. He got around pretty good for a sixty year old, unlike her father whose body was being taken over by rheumatoid arthritis. George was busy talking with French archeologist Andre Jacques, one of the members of their group.

Andre was born and raised in France, but migrated to the United States during his early twenties. He was smart and witty, and a bit of a tease. All the female professors just loved his Maurice Chevalier accent and little mustache that he twirled when he was nervous. He was single like the rest of them but was searching for just the right woman to give birth to a brood of kids when he eventually turned forty and was ready to settle down. That was about a month away and he hadn't settled on one particular woman yet. The other member, Nicholas Stewart was busy on the computer. Nicholas was a graduate assistant like her. He had somehow managed to be in every class that she took, and they even graduated together. Now she wasn't stupid. She knew that he cared for her. In fact, maybe even was in love with her. Unfortunately, she felt nothing but sisterly affection for the tall, curly-hair computer expert. All three men looked up as she approached.

"How was shopping?" George asked as he cleared a chair for her.

"Okay, except for I nearly got trampled by a couple of horses."

"What? How'd that happen?"

"I was just standing in the bazaar minding my own business when these two men rode by trying to escape two police officers. They got away, but I ended up flat on my ass after knocking over a cart of perfume."

Nicholas struggled to keep the smile from his face as he looked down at the computer monitor.

"Go ahead and laugh. I know you want to, but it wasn't funny when it was happening."

Andre patted her hand. "Ah mon petite, everything always happens to you." He rubbed his butt mockingly.

"Not my fault. Anyway, the bandits got away and the police were real nice and concerned about my welfare."

"Bandits?" Nicholas asked. "I just got through reading an article about this guy named Al-Shar Khan."

She sprung to her feet and hurried over to the computer. "That's his name. What does it say about him?"

Nicholas found the site again. "Al-Shar Khan, the hero of the people, is wanted in the connection with grave robbing, and other numerous crimes. No one knows exactly who he is or where he's from. Eye-witnesses can only identify him by his eyes, which are dark, angry, and piercing."

"What else?"

"Nothing else. He's just some local hood who has nothing better to do with his time." He looked puzzled. "You sound like you're interested in him."

Oh, oh, I've hit a nerve. I'd better back off. "No reason. I've never met a bandit before."

Nicholas closed the site. "And hope you never do. He's not going to be anything like those men you've read about in those romance novels you always have your head buried in during your break. Beautiful it may seem, but Egypt is a hard place. It has its share of supremacists and criminal elements who wouldn't hesitate to slit your throat at a drop of a hat."

Bethany went back to her seat. "What are you guys doing?"

George pushed a cup of coffee toward her.

"No thanks," she replied. "It's too darn hot."

"We're mapping out our itinerary while waiting for Hathor El Baz to get back with me with the name of our guide." El Baz was also an archeologist and a dear friend of George. The two of them met at the University of Indianapolis during an anthropology lecture. He had jumped at Hathor's offer to come to Egypt for the dig.

"Did you tell him that the guide has to speak English as well as translate Arabic?"

George nodded. "Yes Miss, why do I have to take an Arabic language class?"

She rolled her eyes at him. "I learned a couple of words and phrases."

"But not enough to communicate with the Cairns," Andre reminded her. "What if you get lost?"

"I can read a compass, and the furthest I plan to go alone is down to the street market. Other than that, I plan to stick by you guys like glue."

George grunted. "You'd better. I promised your father that I would look after you."

"He still thinks I'm a little girl."

"He's just concerned. Egypt is a long way from Indianapolis."

"I'll call him later and let him know we've arrived safely. I hate this time zone. It's too confusing. We're awake and they're asleep back home."

"Don't tell him about the bandits," Andre added. "The man would be on a plane in a second to hunt the scoundrels down."

Bethany chuckled. Everyone knew and loved her father Ernest. He was retired now, but he was once one of the greatest archeologists in the country, and a legend as a professor at the University of Indianapolis. "I won't." She looked down at the maps. "I can't wait to get to the Valley of the Kings."

"We're doing the pyramid tour tonight and we'll meet with the guide later."

The telephone rang and George got up to answer it. He returned a few minutes later. "That was Hathor. He's found us a guide. His name is Feneas and he's knows the desert like the back of his hand."

"Sounds perfect," Bethany agreed absently as her mind wandered back to the bazaar and those gorgeous dark eyes. "Maybe we should have some security in case those bandits show up again."

George nodded as he rolled up the maps. "I'm way ahead of you. That was a part of the deal we made with the Egyptian government. They will be sending two police with us for our protection."

"Maybe they'll send the cute one from this morning."

Nicholas raised his head up from the monitor again. "What cute one from this morning?"

Bethany blushed. "Oh, I left that part out. He came to my rescue after the bandits tried to run me over."

"All the young men back at the university will be disappointed if you find love in Egypt." George always teased her about how crowded the archeologist class was now that she was one of the new professors.

"No, they won't."

Nicholas agreed. "There weren't any hot young things like you teaching when I was in school."

Bethany tossed a pencil at him. "I'm a hot young thing with a brain."

Andre sided with her. "That you are, Mademoiselle Dailet. The youngest professor in the country with a killer rack."

"You guys are the worst. I don't know why I agreed to accompany the three of you here."

George tousled her blonde hair on the way back to his seat. "Because you wouldn't have missed this opportunity for anything in the world. You were born to be an archeologist. It's in your blood."

"That's true. I would have stowed away in one of your suitcases if you wouldn't have offered to take me along."

Andre rose. "Enough of this chit-chat. I'm starving. Let's go eat street."

〜

Eating street, Bethany discovered meant standing up eating next to a meal cart. Not that she was complaining. The grilled chicken she devoured was prepared with just the right amount of cilantro and other spices. George and Andre lunched on lamb shish kabobs accompanied by greens, tomato salad, tahini sauce and pita bread, while Nicholas had a salad of tomato, coriander, mint, green peppers and onions. Afterwards he popped a couple of mints and antacids to ward off the offending aroma.

Later that evening she changed into a comfortable pantsuit and hat and joined the gang for the pyramid tour, which simply took her breath away. Amazed at the fact that the pyramid had been constructed with primitive tools and still existed. Inside the pyramid, she admired the intricate drawings. Bethany bombarded the guide with questions. Her exuberance, she discovered, had an odd effect on Nicholas who smiled at her like a silly lovesick school boy and watched her even when he thought she wasn't watching him.

Hathor El Baz met up with them later for dinner, and he brought along Feneas so they could meet him before they traveled to Luxor together tomorrow. Hathor, like George was in his sixties. But when he wasn't busy exploring old tombs, he kept himself busy by working at the Cairo Antiquities Museum or with the historical library in Luxor.

Feneas was a tall string bean of a fellow with long black hair, and just the beginning of the traditional facial mustache and goatee. He was dressed in a white tunic atop a pair of white pants. His English was accented but clearly understandable, but he seemed almost shy when talking to her. Bethany guessed his age to be around nineteen, which made him the youngest member of their little motley group. He was cute, but too young for her. After dinner, they all crawled into a taxi and went back to the hotel, where they finalized their plans for the next day. Hathor was to accompany them to Luxor, but he had a very important meeting to attend to, so they were going to be pretty much on their own on the first day. Bethany crawled into the bed somewhere around ten but tossed and turned for a couple of hours until the excitement about the trip died down.

CHAPTER 3

*D*awn came too early. Bethany crawled out of the bed and dragged herself into the showers. Less than an hour later, she was dressed in a pair of khaki cargo pants, a khaki camp shirt and a pair of tennis shoes. All her things were packed and just in time for the bellhop to arrive and take them down to one of the waiting four-wheel drives Feneas had rented for their journey. The others, she discovered were similarly dressed in light-colored clothing and hats to ward off the intense heat. They had a quick breakfast in the hotel restaurant and then checked out. Hathor, Andre and George rode in one car, while she, Nicholas and Feneas rode in another. Their luggage and equipment was being driven there by two other guides, and the final car contained two uniformed police officers.

It took several hours to reach Luxor and Bethany felt that she had seen enough sand to last a lifetime. Her spirits perked up once they arrived at the bungalow where they would be staying. The place was huge and beautifully decorated in Egyptian artifacts and furniture. She was shown to her room which thankfully had its own private bath. After a quick change, Feneas took them to their first destination…the Valley of the Kings.

Bethany's heart raced as the line they stood in moved. She and the others waited patiently for their turn to enter the tomb of Ramesses VI.

"We're almost in," André announced. "They only allow in a certain amount of people during the afternoon."

Bethany hoped they all got a chance to go in together. They were on the west bank of the Nile in a valley across from the Thebes where the majority of the royal tombs were located…officially called the Royal Necropolis. She reached down and got a handful of soil to examine. It contained bits of limestone, sedimentary rock and a softer substance called marl. She let it trickle from her hands. The line inched forward. "It's our turn."

The guide counted people while collecting tickets. "The tour will begin in a few minutes," she announced. Moments later they followed her inside. What little air there was, quickly disappeared. The guide explained the rules, including the one about no picture taking which met with a lot of grumbling until she explained that they were trying to make sure that the tombs stay intact for future generations to enjoy. She took them through a long, inclined rock cut corridor, which made a ninety degree turn about fifteen minutes into their tour. It was so hot that Bethany and the others took frequent sips from their water supply. "I would like to tell you that Ramesses VI did not build his own tomb. I don't know why, maybe he was lazy, but this particular tomb was built by his brother, Ramesses V." They walked a little further. "Notice the wall decorations which provide the origins of the heavens, the earth and the creation of the sun."

Bethany noted that the tomb did not have the traditional stairways as most tombs were supposed to have. They went through three corridors that led to the ritual shaft, and then past a four pillared hall, another two corridors, a vestibule and finally the burial chamber. She found the last corridor quite unique, because the floors slope under a horizontal roof. The tour guide explained that it was built that way to keep it from running into part of tomb KV12. Through each passage the ceilings were decorated with astronomical designs and the walls of the first and third corridor had images of the Book of Gates and the Book of Caverns. There were etchings of the king making an offering to Ra-Horakhty, followed by Osiris. In the burial chamber, they finally found the broken sarcophagus of the king.

"Ramesses VI was not found in his tomb," the tour guide explained. "He was found in the tomb of Amenophis II."

"I wonder why?" George asked.

Bethany shrugged her shoulders. "Probably moved there by looters."

Later Feneas took them to where they would be working. It was on the east bank on the opposite side of the Valley of the Kings. "It's hotter than hell here," Bethany replied, removing her hat and mopping her brow with her hand.

Jacques laughed. "How do you know how hot hell is?"

She replaced the hat and moved a step or two away from where she stood to get a better dirt sample from the cliff. "I've been there a couple of times, believe me." Her feet sank down into the sand.

"This is Egypt. What did you expect?"

"A cool breeze every now and then."

"This is, after all, a desert. It's a place of death. Desolate. It's why the spot was chosen."

"This ground is kind of mushy."

George stopped doing what he was doing. "Mushy?"

"Yeah, like my feet are sinking."

The other men froze. "Don't move," Andre cautioned her.

Too late.

Bethany was already in motion. "What are you guys talking about?" The ground opened up as she shifted her weight. "Oh, oh." Her entire body disappeared beneath the earth as a big hole appeared. "Help!" Darkness engulfed her on the way down. The hat flew from her head and her blouse freed itself as she descended. Air left her lungs as her body moved downward. Her feet hit something so hard that it jarred her knees. Bethany sank down as pain shot up her legs. She closed her eyes and then reopened them. Tiny shafts of light illuminated the hole allowing her a little comfort. Someone called her name from a distance high above. She didn't know how far she had fallen but she knew she couldn't get out without assistance.

"Bethany, can you hear me?"

It was George. "Yes," she shouted as she sat on the ground.

"Are you injured?"

"I don't think so. Just a few bumps and bruises. I won't be able to tell until I try to stand."

"I've sent for help. Try not to move around."

Dust and debris fell down the hole on top of her. She brushed it out of her hair. "I'll try."

"Do you have enough water?"

She had a full bottle in her waist pack. "Yes, but there's no rest room down here."

There was a chuckle in the distance.

"Can you see anything?"

"What's there to see? I'm in a hole." She focused. There was something solid in front of her…like a wall. Something on it glimmered like gold. "Maybe I'm hallucinating," she muttered. "No, there is definitely something there." More dust and debris rained down on her. She waited until it cleared to focus again. The hole she had fallen in was much larger than she thought at first. Either she was in a tunnel or a very dark walkway. It was probably something left over from an ancient city. There were many places around the world built on top of other cities.

The voices from up above returned. This time it was Andre. "The police sent for an emergency vehicle. It's on its way. It might take a little while."

"I've got no place to go."

He laughed. "Keep up the good spirits."

Even from that distance, she could hear the concern in his voice. She looked over at the wall again. There was a sign, like a plaque. Curiosity got the better of her. Bethany rose. Her knees ached but not enough to hinder movement. She took that as a sign to go forward toward the wall.

"It is a plaque." She squinted to make out the etching. "Beware." She frowned. "Oh great. Beware what? Amasis. Beware, something, something Amasis. Doesn't make sense to me."

She ran her hand over the etching. The plaque set against something solid. It was huge and it was separated into two parts…like doors. "It is doors. Big doors." She pulled on one of them. Something clicked. "Let me try this again." More debris fell on her as the door moved. "Yeah," she said triumphantly. A damp, musty smell filtered out of the opening. She tried to pull the door again, but it wouldn't budge. "Maybe I can peep inside. No, too dark."

"Bethany, can you hear us?"

"Yes."

"They're sending down a long rope ladder."

"Darn." She wanted desperately to know what was behind the doors.

"Here it comes." Something swooshed above her and then it rattled along the dirt walls. "Do you see it?"

Bethany moved away from the doors and felt along the walls until her hand made contact with the ladder. "I have it." It was made of some kind of braided material, and luckily long enough to reach her. "Make sure you guys are holding on. I'm coming up." She moved up the rungs, looking down one last time at the doors with disappointment. Five or ten minutes later, she was back on land being tended to by some EMTs far away from the spot where she had fallen. George and the other men hovered around her.

"Are you sure you're okay?" Nicholas asked her repeatedly.

"Yes, just a little dirty."

One of the paramedics looked into her eyes with the tiny light. He felt along her legs to see if she had any broken bones. Nicholas kept a firm eye on the paramedic to make sure he wasn't touching anything on Bethany he shouldn't.

"She's fine," the paramedic assured him. "And very lucky." He finished with her, packed up his things, and said goodbye to them and the officers. "Be careful," he told her as he drove away. The rest of the tourists and gawkers were gone now that she was safely out of the hole and in no apparent trouble. The police left a few minutes later.

"I guess we should get back to work," George said as Bethany rose.

"It's too hot," Bethany protested as she pulled her water bottle from her pack. "And I've lost my hat."

Andre pulled a second hat from his pack. "How many times have I told you to always be prepared, Mademoiselle?"

She kissed him on the cheek. "You're a lifesaver."

"Now drink your water and let's get back to work, woman."

Bethany took a sip and replaced the cap. "I have something to tell you guys."

"I think she's procrastinating," Nicholas joked.

"No, I'm serious. I saw something while I was down in the hole that you're never going to believe."

George turned to her. "Something like what?"

"A room. It's buried beneath the ground. It has a gold sign with Arabic writing on it."

"Are you sure you didn't hit your head on the way down?" Nicholas asked teasingly.

"No, I landed on my feet like a cat. I also saw two doors."

"What did the sign say?" Andre asked. "Oh, what am I asking? You can't read Arabic."

"I could make out the words beware and Amasis."

"I'll look it up." Nicholas popped open his computer hoping to pick up a frequency. "Damn, we're too far out to get the Internet."

George stopped him. "No need for that. I think I know what's down there. What else did you see?"

"Not much. I tried to pull open one of the doors. I loosened it but this funky smell came out and it wouldn't budge."

"A funky smell…like something has been sealed for a very long time?" Andre asked.

Bethany nodded. "Like an old tomb."

"Why didn't you say something earlier?"

"Because there were too many people around, and I didn't want to look stupid in front of the police if it wasn't so."

Nicholas sat down on the ground in shock. "Just think of the ramifications if it is an undiscovered tomb down there. You'll be famous."

Bethany shook her head. "No, we'll be famous. It's all for one and one for all."

"Except if it's not a tomb," he corrected. "Then you'll look stupid by yourself. Right fellows?"

"Oh, yes, yes," Andre agreed.

Bethany smiled. "With friends like you guys who needs enemies?"

CHAPTER 4

"*W*hat did you see?"

Jamaal folded up the binoculars and handed them over to Al-Shar. "Four people. Three males and a female. I think they're Americans but I can't be too sure from this distance."

Al took the binoculars and trained them down on wadi. "I believe you're right. I wondered what happened. An emergency vehicle means trouble."

"You know tourists. Someone probably passed out from the heat. They were hovering over the female a moment ago."

"She looks fine to me."

"Hopefully and not some scoundrels out to make a buck by stealing artifacts."

Al nodded. That was a possibility. There had been a lot of that over the last few centuries and he planned to put a stop to it. Looters had damaged or destroyed a lot of the archeological sites, robbing their people of their pasts. There was a big demand for artifacts. He meant to stop illicit trade between the smugglers and the private collectors who paid top dollar for what they could get their hands on.

"What are they doing now?"

"They're looking down on the ground at something. Probably a map."

"There isn't anything of any value buried there," Jamaal replied. "The royal tombs are in the East Valley."

"Maybe they're anthropologists, or they're studying the environment." He certainly hoped they were. It would make his job a lot easier.

"Maybe. Do you think we need to go down and have a look?"

"Not just yet. I need to study them for a while." *There is something vaguely familiar about the female.*

Jamaal leaned against the cliff. "It's about to reach the hottest part of the day. I don't know about you, but I have grown accustomed to being inside at this time, where it's cool."

"You're such a wimp."

"I am not. Can I help it if I do my best work after dark?"

"This is true. Just give me a few minutes and then we'll get the horses and ride down into the wadi on our way back home." He looked back through the binoculars training them on the woman. He didn't need the binoculars to tell that she was a female. There were just too many curves. "I think I've seen enough. Let's get home before I parch."

Bethany looked up at the approaching riders as she surveyed the area. "We have company," she announced to the others. Two men on horses stopped several feet away from them. George and Andre left their equipment and walked cautiously over to them. Bethany tried to get a good look at who they were but the sun blinded her vision when she stared up. After a few minutes of conversing, the two men rode off and George and Andre returned.

"What did they want?" Nicholas asked.

"They were just asking about what happened earlier. They saw the commotion from up in the cliffs but just managed to get down. One of them said they were just passing by to see if they could be of any assistance."

"Mighty nice of them," Bethany replied getting back to work. "I hope you didn't make me sound like a total klutz."

Nicholas chuckled. "Well, you are."

"No, we didn't," George replied. "One of them seemed very concerned. He said the valley was much too dangerous for a woman."

Bethany frowned. "Chauvinist."

"I think we need to call it a day," George announced several hours later. "We need to get back to the bungalow and to make some decisions."

The rest of them agreed. Feneas had returned along with the other drivers from the tourist center and less than an hour later all of the equipment was packed and they were headed for home.

"Nice of you to join us, Your Highness," Queen Naadirah said to her son when he entered the throne room.

Yahi bowed before his parents. "Sorry, being a prince has put many demands on my time."

"How was your trip?" His father, King Waheed asked as Yahi joined them. His younger sister Kasia nodded at him and smirked skeptically at his excuse.

"Most productive. Emir Hatem sends warm regards."

"I hope you invited your god-father to join us for our anniversary celebration," his mother replied.

"Yes, I did. He accepted. I am going to pay him a visit again soon." Yahi sat down on his throne. "What is on the agenda for today?"

"Same old things. We have a few guests arriving from the Nubian kingdom, followed by the arrival of the new president of the United States and his family."

Yahi rolled his eyes up at the ceiling. "Not another political conference."

"Better get used to it," his father warned. "You will be king one day so look at this at practice."

"Yes, father. I shall try to keep from passing out from boredom."

Kasia giggled. "Maybe Yahi has better things to do with his time like romancing some pure young maiden."

Yahi scowled at her. "No, I do not little sister."

"Having a dry spell, my brother?"

"No, just not in a relationship at the moment, if it's any of your business."

The queen had had enough. "Stop the bickering. You two act like a couple of babies sometimes."

Kasia poked her tongue at him. Yahi pulled a lock of her long brown hair. At twenty-five, Kasia bore an amazing resemblance to their mother. They were both very tall and beautiful women who possessed an excellent sense of humor as well as being scholarly and worldly. She, like him had been tutored most of their childhood and then sent away to universities in the United States to broaden their horizons. She had developed a passion for western world fashion and the Internet, while he had learned that there was more to life than just sitting around a palace being worshipped by subjects.

"What happened to that English princess you were dating?" his father asked as the Nubian guests were announced.

"We decided it was best that we just remain friends," Yahi lied.

"Are you ever going to find a young woman and settle down?" his mother asked, putting her welcome face on.

Not likely, he thought. He found the idea of being shackled to one woman repulsive. Why settle for one when there were millions from which to choose?

Bethany took a nice cool shower, threw on a pair of comfortable cotton shorts and a tank top. She would have preferred to omit the bra, but she was the lone female in a group of single males, so it wasn't feasible to be free no matter how perky her bosoms were. Feneas had gone to visit some relatives for the rest of the afternoon and would be returning the next evening to take them back to the site. They had a lot of planning to do, and calls to make. Hathor had joined them at the bungalow and was quite taken back when George told him of Bethany's find. He had been on the phone putting out a few feelers, but not enough to leak anything to the public.

"There shouldn't be anything in that quadrant," he said later after they had been perusing maps of the area.

"But that doesn't mean there's nothing there," Bethany reasoned. "You'll see for yourself tomorrow when you go down into that hole."

"Did you make sure that the area has been sealed and secured?" Andre asked Hathor.

"I have people there as we speak. They're very discrete."

"That's comforting to know."

"What about equipment?" Nicholas asked. "We're going to need some rope ladders and hard hats with lights."

"Part of my job, or have you forgotten that I've only been doing this for the last thirty years?"

"Sorry. I'm just so excited. Never in my wildest dreams could I imagine being a part of what's about to happen."

"We need you focused, young man. Get on that computer contraption and dig up everything you can on that area."

"What do you want me to do?" Bethany asked. She was tired of just sitting around and anxious to get her hands dirty.

"Help Nicholas. I'll take George and Andre with me to help carry some things."

"But Nicholas is younger than I am," George replied candidly.

Hathor smirked and put his hat back on. "Do you know anything about surfing the net for information?"

"I can find the university website," George said.

"Not the same thing, my friend. Leave the internet to the kids."

Nicholas positioned the magnetometer against the ground searching for deviations in the Earth's magnetic field beneath the ground where Bethany had fallen. It picked up something instantly. "There's something there," he announced to the others.

"See, I told you," Bethany bragged. "Hallucination my butt."

George and Hathor joined them while Andre kept watch for any interlopers.

"Can you tell what it is?" Hathor asked.

"Not yet, but it's giving off a very high reading." He paused. "It's big."

George looked down at the meter and whistled. "I wonder how much territory it covers."

Nicholas scratched his head. "Hard to say."

"The only way we're going to find out is by going down there," Hathor answered. "The sooner the better." He walked toward the ladder. "Come on. Let's go."

Nicholas and George hurried behind him. The plan was for the two older men to go down into the hole while Andre and Nicholas held on to the ladder. Bethany was to act as lookout and warn them should anyone approach. Andre slipped over to give Nicholas a hand. A few minutes later the two men disappeared beneath the earth.

The wait was agonizing, Bethany discovered as she paced around. They had been down maybe an hour when George's head came out of the hole. The rest of the body and Hathor followed. Bethany hurried over. "Well?"

"George hugged her. "Congratulations kid, you've hit pay dirt."

Bethany squealed. "Really?"

"Yes, really," Hathor answered, dusting off his pants. "It's a tomb alright, and you found it."

Nicholas laughed. "Whoopee. We're going to be famous."

"The toast of Egypt," Andre agreed.

"How soon can we start the excavation?" Bethany asked once George released her from the bear hug.

"Whoa. We got to get past the red tape. We got to let my associates know over at the Supreme Council of Antiquities and then they have to come and see for themselves, and give their permission for us to begin. They'll bring their people in on it. There are so many things to prepare, so get ready to work hard."

"I'm freezing," Bethany said to Nicholas after the two of them had returned to their seats after dancing. The air-conditioning seemed to seep through the sporty pantsuit she had just purchased for the party to celebrate their historical find. "I think I might step outside just to warm up a bit."

Nicholas rose. "Do you want me to accompany you?"

"No, you stay and enjoy the fun. I'll be okay and only be gone a few minutes." She rose and walked across the small ballroom to the exit door, took the elevator down to the lobby and walked out the front door. The heat hit her like a ton of bricks. Usually, back home in Indianapolis, there was a cool breeze around this time of night. She didn't think she'd felt a breeze the whole while she was in Egypt. She sat down on a bench. It was unusually quiet. Getting too warm for comfort, she decided to go back in. Two masked men stepped from behind a bush and pointed guns in her face.

"Please come with us," one of them said.

"I don't have any money, so if you're planning to rob me you're wasting your time."

"We do not seek money, just you," the larger of the two men said.

"What if I refuse?"

He cocked the gun. "Then this is an offer you can't refuse."

Bethany rose, looking around for help. The chances of someone appearing in the lobby were slim to none since the reservation office was on the third floor of the hotel just like the one back in Cairo.

"Don't waste your time. There is no one around to save you."

The one who hadn't spoken nodded in agreement. He looked her over from head to toe and said something to the other man in Arabic.

"Yes, she will do nicely." He snatched her from in front of the hotel, tossed her over his shoulder, and made a mad dash around the side of the hotel. "If you scream I will kill you," he said as they made it to a car stored in a dark area of the parking lot. He tossed her into the back and crawled in beside her. The other man climbed into the front seat, started the engine and drove away quickly. The one beside her jerked her shoulders as she tried to hop out. He bound her hands and then her feet with rope.

She gasped. "Where are you taking me?"

"That is no concern of yours."

"Excuse me, but I beg to differ since you're kidnapping me." She decided not to struggle since it was useless and she didn't want to get shot. Her purse containing her cell phone and her identification were locked up in her room so she couldn't contact anyone if she ever got her hands free again. She decided to just play it cool and hoped it would all turn out for the better. Something sharp pieced her shoulder. "Ouch, what is that?"

"Just a little something to make you sleep."

"You bastard. You shot me with drugs?"

"Go to sleep beautiful one, I'm tired of hearing you speak."

Grogginess came over her quickly, rending her immobile and sleepy. Her last thoughts were of praying she wouldn't be gang-raped and murdered. It would devastate her father.

~

Mark Kauffman stood in the den of the illustrious archeologist, Ernest Dailet, awaiting the older man's presence. He had not seen him in months since he and Bethany had ended their relationship, but just stopped by to make him an offer he couldn't refuse…an opportunity to invest in his latest business endeavor. He had been turned down by all his other potential clients and Ernest was his last hope. The elder Dailet entered looking a lot feebler than he had the last time he saw him. Mark rose and helped him into a seat.

"Thank you, my boy. These old legs don't work as well as they used to. Arthritis is a bitch."

"Would you like me to fix you a drink?"

"Scotch," Ernest replied. "No rocks." He chuckled at the old man's archeology joke even though he had heard it a thousand times. He walked over to the bar, fixed two drinks and carried it over to Ernest. "How is Bethany?"

"She's fine. She's on an archeology dig."

"In Indianapolis?"

Ernest laughed. "Oh no. The only old fossil around here is me. No, she's in Egypt with George Eisemann and a few of their colleagues."

Mark whistled. "She must be elated. It's a dream come true for her." *Damn*. Deep down inside he was disappointed because he planned to use her to convince her father to invest in the business. Of course, there really wasn't a business, but Ernest wouldn't find that out before it was too late.

"She sounded as happy as a clam the last time I talked to her."

"How long is she supposed to be gone?"

"About a month or two, depending on what they find."

This will not do. That's much too long. He would be put out of his house and his office by then. "I'm glad for her. It's something she's always wanted to do."

"Well, what brings you all the way over to this side of town?"

"I was in the neighborhood," Mark lied. "I had a business meeting nearby."

"A business meeting this time of night?"

"Yes, it's the only time the clients could meet with me. I'm thinking about erecting a shopping mall nearby and it was a meeting with a couple of investors."

Ernest sipped his drink. "How did it go?"

"Fine, except that I still need a few backers to get the ball rolling."

"Tell me some more about it. I'm always interested in investing."

Mark's hopes brightened. *This is going to be easier than I thought.* He rattled out his plans to Ernest for over an hour. "I just need some more up front capital to get the ball rolling."

Ernest didn't say anything for a while as he thought over the idea.

"What do you think?" Mark asked.

"Sounds like a very profitable idea."

"Do you really think so?"

Ernest nodded.

"Would you be interested in investing?"

"No way."

The smile disappeared from Mark's face. "What do you mean, no way?"

Ernest laughed. "I might be old, Mark, but I can smell a scam from a mile away."

"It isn't a scam. This is a legitimate business venture."

"I've heard it all before. Bethany told me everything."

Mark nibbled at his bottom lip. *This is not going at all the way I planned. I just expected the rich old coot to agree and just write me a check.* "Everything like what?"

"Like how you bilked so many people out of their money on your last scheme that they wanted to run you out of town."

"That's not true. I just had a couple of set-backs."

"And let's not forget that building over on Elm that you never completed or paid the contractors. I passed it just the other day. It's an eyesore."

"That's not true either. Bethany was just exaggerating."

"My daughter does not exaggerate. She's just a bit of a romantic fool for staying with you as long as she did. You think I've forgotten what you did to her? You left her for another woman whose father was a tad bit richer than I was. Well, I guess the joke was on you when you found out that her family was nearly destitute from bad business deals."

Mark balled up his fists. "How dare you accuse me of such ungentle-manly acts? Bethany and I parted on friendly terms. It was a mutual agreement between the two of us."

"You can say what you want because Bethany is not here to say otherwise. So what did you come over here for—to sweet talk her into asking me to give you the money?"

"Yes."

"Well, that's the first honest thing that came out of your mouth since you arrived. I'm so glad that you called the engagement off before you took me and my daughter to the cleaners. Now I think it's about time for you to leave."

Mark put down his drink, pissed by his humiliation and outsmarted by the old man. "You're wrong. I loved Bethany. In fact, I still do."

"Well, she doesn't love you anymore. I think this little trip is going to get you completely out of her system. I hope she finds someone over there who will sweep her off her feet. I'm kind of partial to that Nicholas fellow she works with."

"That computer geek?"

Ernest nodded. "Fine, strapping young man with all that dark curly hair. They'll make some very cute babies."

"Not if I get to her first."

"What do you mean?"

"I think I'll go over to Egypt and woo her back, maybe even marry her over there."

Ernest rose. "You'll do no such a thing. You stay away from my daughter."

Mark pushed him and Ernest fell, hitting his head against an end table beside the chair.

"Ernest?"

The old man didn't respond. Mark knelt down beside him. He couldn't feel a pulse. "Ernest, are you okay?"

Still no response.

Mark backed toward the door terrified. "I better get out of here before he recovers and calls the police." He ran out the door before anyone could see him and arrest him for murder.

CHAPTER 5

*B*ethany opened her eyes. It was dark and everything was blurry. She struggled to sit and discovered that she was still bound. "Where am I?"

Someone lit a lantern. It was a man. "So you have awakened?"

Bethany focused on his face until she could see most of it clearly. "Now I remember. You kidnapped me from the hotel. Where is your friend?"

"Sabola is making plans for our trip."

"Going someplace?"

"Shortly." He watched her for a few minutes without saying anything. His eyes were dark, but the iris was rimmed in red like he'd been drinking… and not just beer…the hard stuff that was frowned upon in Egypt.

"So what are your plans for me Mr.….? I figure I'd be dead by now if you wanted to kill me."

"Call me Maaches, and I still might do it if you give me too much sass. I plan to use you."

Bethany shrank back. "Use me? You mean rape me?"

Maaches rose and walked over to her. "That thought had crossed my mind. You're a very desirable woman for an American."

Bethany didn't respond. She didn't want to encourage him since his mind was made up. He touched her hair.

"It is soft like satin."

She willed herself not to pull away.

"Lucky for you that I have taken care of that need earlier." He ran his finger down her face. "You will bring a much better price if I deliver you in perfect condition."

"You are going to sell me?"

He laughed. "What did you think? People would pay a lot of money for a woman like you."

"Sell me to whom?" The door to the room opened and Sabola walked in. He looked at the two of them questionably like he thought something was going on between them. He said something to Maaches and then the two of them argued for a couple of seconds.

Maaches turned to her. "Come, it's time to go." He lifted her and tossed her over his shoulders again.

"I feel like a sack of potatoes. I can walk you know."

"You might try to run away if I untie you and I can't afford for you to do that. This way is better."

He carried her out of the room and up a flight of stairs. It was hot wherever they were. Moments later, they exited and stepped outside. It was dark, which meant either it was still the same night she was kidnapped or the night after. She couldn't tell since she had been drugged.

He carried her back out to the car and dumped her back in. He crawled in beside her like the last time with Sabola driving. She had no idea where they were. Everything outside the windshield just looked strange and things whizzed by making them unrecognizable. A vast amount of time seemed to pass and then they stopped. Sabola got out first, said something and then walked up to a door of a large house. He returned a few minutes later and beckoned for Maaches to follow.

Maaches opened the door and stepped out. Several other men appeared. They talked and then Maaches looked back inside the car. "It is time." He pulled her out and mounted her over his shoulder again. "Try to keep a civil tongue in that pretty little head of yours. In fact, you are not to speak at all."

He stepped inside the house with her, deposited her in a room, and then disappeared. At least she could see this time. The room was nicely painted, with a couple of chairs and a table. Egyptian news played on a portable television on the other side of the room. And the place had air-conditioning.

She continued to look around. The door was near but useless since she was still tied up. It opened a few minutes later and Maaches appeared. He picked her up, carried her out of the room, down a hall and into another room. He unceremoniously dropped her to the floor.

"You could be gentler with her," a deep voice stated.

"Why? She is just a woman."

Bethany rolled her eyes at Maaches but she did not speak or cry out in pain.

"A beautiful woman but very opinionated. She is well worth what I'm asking as long as she doesn't speak."

The other man laughed. "I'm not bargaining until I get a good look at what you're offering. All I can see is the back of her head."

Maaches flipped Bethany over with his foot, as if she was a piece of carpet. Dark alluring eyes stared down at her in shock and disbelief. The rest of his face was still covered but she'd recognize those eyes anywhere. They belonged to the bandit, Al-Shar Khan.

"So, what do you think?" Maaches asked.

Al-Shar's eyes ran over her body possessively. "We have a deal."

Maaches clapped his hands excitedly. "I knew she was worth it the moment I saw her standing outside the hotel. You are a very lucky man."

Bethany scrambled to a seated position and stared questionably at both men. "You sold me to a bandit, Maaches? What do you get in return?"

"Ten Arabian stallions…the best in the country."

"Now where would a common thief get ten Arabian stallions? You better make sure he's not trying to swindle you."

Both men laughed. Maaches spoke to him in Arabic. Maaches pulled her hair. "Didn't I ask you not to speak woman? Al-Shar Khan is not a common criminal. He is well known and respected amongst our people. Everyone knows that he has the best horses in the world. Why in the hell do you think we went to all this trouble to get something worth trading?"

"Because you're a common thief too. No, you're worse. You're a kidnapper."

Al-Shar nudged her with his sandaled feet. Bethany looked at him angrily. "Keep your feet off me. I am not a dog."

"Feisty," Al-Shar replied. "I don't know, Maaches. I think you got the better end of the deal."

Maaches looked shocked. "Why would you say that?"

"You have ten horses while I seem to have a woman who has a penchant for getting herself into dangerous situations."

So he did recognize her. "I do not. I just happened to be in the wrong place at the wrong time."

He laughed. "You don't have to worry about that anymore. I will make sure that you are safe and sound."

"Does that mean you are going to return me back to my friends and family?"

"No. Why would I do a foolish thing like that? I traded good horseflesh for you. You will have a new life now as part of my harem." Maaches and Sabola rose. "A deal is a deal, Al-Shar. When can we get the horses?"

"Right now, if you like." He clapped his hands and another masked Egyptian appeared. He looked a bit familiar too, but she couldn't be sure.

"Take these men to the stables and give them their horses."

The other man bowed and beckoned for the kidnappers to follow them. They left, leaving her alone with the bandit. She found him staring down at her with a little too much interest. "I don't know why our paths have been crossing so much lately, but I mean to get to the bottom of it."

"Coincidence," Bethany replied.

"I don't believe in coincidences. Are you a spy?"

Bethany sputtered. "A what?"

"Who are you working for? Is it Maaches? I may trade with him, but that doesn't mean I trust him."

"Now why would I want to work for him? The man just kidnapped me and traded me to you for ten damned horses."

"Thoroughbred horses," he corrected.

"You're missing the point. I am not a spy, and I demand that you take me back to my hotel in Luxor."

"Can't do that. Not even if I wanted to, which I don't."

"Are you afraid that the police will capture you and put you in jail for looting, and let's not mention bartering in female slave trade?"

"Yes, so you see I can't take you back. You will just lead them back here to me."

"I don't even know where here is, and as far as this spy business goes, I am an archeologist."

"You will stay in my harem until I can prove you're not a spy. By the way, what is your name? I don't think just calling you woman is appropriate."

"It's Bethany Dailet. I'm from a place called Indianapolis in the United States, where I'm a professor at a university."

"I'll check it out."

"And then you'll let me go?"

Al-Shar laughed, clapped his hands, and had her carried out by two very big, extremely handsome eunuchs.

Jamaal entered the room after he was sure that the woman was gone. "What have you gotten us into now, my friend? First, we're bartering with thieves, and we're kidnapping women and holding them hostage."

Al shrugged his shoulders. "How was I supposed to know that Maaches would bring a woman here to trade for horses?"

"He's a crook. That should have been your first clue."

Al arrogantly waved off the sarcasm.

"And isn't she the same woman from the bazaar and also the one from Luxor?"

"Yes, I think she's a spy. There's no way this could just be a coincidence."

"Maybe it is. Maybe fate has put her in your path for a reason."

"She cost me ten horses."

Jamaal frowned. "Come on, she's worth more than that and you know it."

"Well, maybe fifteen, or maybe not even that much. She's such a sassy little thing with those big blue eyes and full luscious lips."

Jamaal chuckled. "I knew it."

"What did you know?"

"That you're attracted to her."

"I am not. I'm just saying she's very beautiful for an American."

"So, what are you going to do now, return her?"

"In time," Al replied. "I need to find out first if she is who she says she is."

"What do you mean she's missing?" George asked Nicholas as the party came to an end.

"She went outside to get warm and she never returned."

"How long ago was this?" Andre asked springing to his feet.

"About an hour ago. I went out to look for her but I can't find her."

"Did you check her room?"

Nicholas nodded. "It's empty."

"This is not good," George said as he nervously paced the floor. "Maybe we ought to call the police."

"I'll take care of that," Hathor volunteered. "I have a friend on the force. I'm just hoping she's in a deli in the hotel or something."

"I have the security pulling the surveillance video to see if someone came up while she was outside," Nicholas told them. "Bethany is a pretty level headed young woman. She wouldn't just go off with someone she didn't know."

George patted him on the shoulder to comfort him. "We all know how you feel about her. She's like a daughter to me. We'll find her."

"You think one of us should call her father?" Andre asked.

George shook his head. "No, it's too soon, and we don't want to worry Ernest unnecessarily. Let's give it twenty-four hours. If we haven't found her by then I'll call him."

CHAPTER 6

"You are to sleep here," one of the huge eunuchs said to her after she was led away from Al-Shar.

"Thanks, but I won't be here long."

One of them removed the ropes from her hands and feet.

"Oh, no. Where do you plan to go?" he asked. He was big, bald and had an eloquent voice like a Shakespearian actor. Even his muscles had muscles.

"Home," she replied. "Al-Shar Khan will come to his senses. He can't keep me here against my will."

The other man was also big and tall, but not as muscular. He made up for it by being devilishly handsome with dark brown hair, and twinkling doe eyes. "Al-Shar can do anything he pleases to do," he told her. "This is his home and his land."

"How can a thief have so much property?" She rubbed her sore wrists.

The two men looked at each other oddly and the smaller one shrugged his shoulders.

"Al-Shar is not a thief. He is a good and fair man."

"He just purchased me for ten horses. That's illegal in my country."

"You're no longer in your country. That is a fair price for a dowry."

"A dowry? A dowry? We're not engaged. He traded two other crooks ten horses for me and then he threw me in this harem with you guys."

The big one laughed. "Ten horses. You must be very good."

"I am not."

Several very beautiful women passed the door giggling.

The large one sighed with a mixture of delight and remorse as one waved to him. "You can be in a place worse than this."

"What is your name?"

"I am called Jabari," the big one answered. "And he is Kesi. We guard Al-Shar's harem."

Another scantily dressed woman passed by and winked at Jabari.

Bethany looked down below the two men's waists for some kind of reaction to all the jiggling flesh they were admiring. Nothing. Not even a slow rise. Hell, she was a woman and even she was a bit turned on by what the woman was offering. How could they stand being so near, yet never being able to sample? "What do the guardians of the harem do?"

Jabari took his eyes off the woman. She disappeared behind a door across the hall. "We keep men out and women in."

"We also watch over the women and keep them from squabbling," Kesi explained.

Bethany raised an eyebrow. "They fight?"

Kesi nodded.

"What about?"

"About who is the prettiest, and who should get to sleep with Al-Shar Khan."

"Ugg. Too much info." She could imagine what that was like. Cat fighting, hair pulling, with the victor trembling beneath him, and watching his eyes change from dark to smoky. "So, what am I supposed to do while I wait my turn to be ravished by his Excellency?"

Jabari walked over to a chair and picked up a bundle of clothes. "First you are to bathe, and then change into these. Then you will come back here and be introduced to the rest of the women. You'll eat, bathe, socialize, and work with them and if you survive the first week without being killed or trying to escape you'll be accorded thirty minutes outside the harem for some exercise."

It sounded like a prison to her, no matter how he tried to nice it up. He clapped his hands and two women appeared. "This is Eboni and Lotus." The two women looked at her with caution. "Stop staring. You'll frighten her off." Both women snapped to attention. "This is…" he paused. "Pardon me; I forgot to ask your name."

"Bethany Dailet."

"Dailet, Dailet, where have I heard that name before?" Kesi asked.

Jabari scratched his bald heard. "It's the name of a fashion designer from France."

"My mother," Bethany replied. "She died a couple of years ago."

"Kesi gushed. "I loved her stuff when I was a young man. She made real cute earrings."

Bethany smirked. *What a perfect waste of man flesh.*

"Please show Bethany to the bathroom," Jabari continued. "She will be staying with us for a while." Both women nodded.

Bethany rose. "What makes you think I won't try to get away?"

Kesi laughed. "One of us would catch you before you made it to the door. We're very good at what we do. Haven't lost a woman yet, and besides, you might grow to like it here. I heard that Al-Shar knows how to please a woman."

Vulgar. "We'll see." She followed Eboni and Lotus out of the room and down a hall to the bathroom. It was huge, but not opulent. Several other women were there talking, but all conversation ceased the moment they entered. Arabic sentences flew at Eboni and Lotus. The two tried to answer the best they could, but the other woman kept bombarding them with more questions. Bethany pulled Lotus on the side. "What are they saying?"

"They want to know who you are and why is your skin like milk and honey?"

She was the lone American chicken in a hen house of Arabic, Egyptian and African females, which meant she stuck out like a sore thumb. Bethany bowed. "Pleased to meet all of you."

Lotus translated. There was more talk and more questions. "They are worried that Al-Shar will not want them after he sees you."

"Please assure them I'm not interest in Al-Shar."

Lotus repeated and the others laughed.

"Why are they laughing?"

"Every woman wants Al-Shar," Eboni explained. "He is the greatest lover in the world."

Bethany exhaled. *How am I going to get myself out of this?*

～

"Stop pacing Nicholas," Hathor ordered. "You're making me dizzy."

"I can't help it. It's been over forty-eight hours. Bethany might be dead for all we know, or lost. She doesn't have a sense of direction, even back in Indianapolis."

"I would laugh if this was not a serious situation. The police are doing everything they can to find her. At least we know she didn't just walk away." The hotel's surveillance video had revealed her being kidnapped by two masked men who drove off in a dark colored car. They couldn't tell the nationality because it was too dark.

"It could be any two men, even the bandit and his friend," Nicholas said.

"The bandit?" Hathor asked.

"Al-Shar Khan. He nearly ran over her in the bazaar the first day we were here."

"I've heard of him. But it's all been good. He is a champion for the poor. He brings them food and supplies."

"The Internet failed to mention that. All I've read is horrible tales about him."

"Don't believe everything you read."

George entered the room. "Did you contact her father?" Andre asked. He had been sitting off by himself staring out the window.

George sat down. "I have some bad news. Ernest is dead."

Nicholas spun around. "What?"

"He's dead. From a head injury. The police thought he passed out at first, but now they think that he's been murdered."

"How horrible. He was one of the finest archeologists in the world," Hathor replied.

"We have to find her now," Nicholas insisted.

"Her brother is posting a reward for her safe return," George informed them.

～

"Thank you, Al-Shar," the young woman said after accepting the sack of food he gave her.

"Do not thank me. There's also something in there for the baby."

The young woman's eyes filled with tears. "You are most generous."

Al crept out of the cemetery. Jamaal waited patiently with the horses. "It is getting late. We must get back before the patrols arrive."

Al agreed, hopped on his horse and then he rode off. Jamaal followed, looking back to make sure the two of them had not been followed. They rode hard until they made it to town, ducking through dark areas to avoid people. They had almost made it back to the bunker when Al stopped to look at something.

"What's wrong?" Jamaal asked turning his horse around.

"It's a reward poster."

"For us?"

"No, for our latest harem guest. So looks like she was telling the truth. She is an archeologist, and someone is offering a big reward for her return."

"I knew you had taken this too far, Al," Jamaal nervously stated. "They're going to throw our asses in jail for kidnapping her."

Al moved the horse away from the poster. "You worry too much. No one can connect her to us." He rode off.

Jamaal pressed his knees into the horse's sides and rode fast to catch up with his friend. "I don't care how pretty she is. She's not worth going to jail for. At least not for kidnapping. I hope you have a plan."

"I always have a plan."

"How come I don't believe you?"

"Because you're a worry wart."

They stabled the horses as soon as they reached the bunker. The two men went down and then took the tunnel to the right to the house they used for their hiding place. Al turned on the television and tried to find any information he could on the kidnapping. He didn't exactly have a plan as he had told Jamaal. All he knew was that he had to get the woman back to her hotel and hoped she could not lead the police back to them.

Maybe being kidnapped and thrown into a harem isn't so bad. Bethany lay submerged up to her neck in a milky bubble bath. The temperature of the water was just warm enough to get rid of the aches and pains of being tied up by Maaches. Eboni and Lotus floated nearby blissfully unashamed of their nakedness. Communal bathing took a little getting used to until she discovered that she had nothing to be ashamed of. So, she had survived her first week. She was given a beautiful room and just light household duties around the harem. She still hadn't made any friends, but she hadn't made any enemies either.

Al watched Bethany, Eboni and Lotus as they played around the bathroom like a bunch of kids. What a glorious sight. Unfortunately, Ms. Dailet had already dressed and was trying to hide the clothes of the delightfully beautiful girls assigned to keep her company.

"No fair, Bethany," Lotus squealed as she climbed out of the bath. Lotus was a third generation harem girl. Part Egyptian and part Japanese, and very limber.

Bethany giggled. "I will return them if you show me how to do my hair so it can be as soft as yours."

They touched each other's hair? Al gulped. He had heard the rumors about what went on in the harem late at night but had never witnessed it because he was always out working. The lovely dark-skinned Eboni stepped out. Her father had sold her to someone when she was ten and she arrived at the harem at sixteen. She was bright and kind and the other women always looked up to her for advice in guidance. Her job was to schedule the work and the nocturnal visits to his room which were becoming few and far between.

He walked away from the steamy window still contemplating what his next move would be with Bethany. He had already put in a call to her father in the United States only to receive the devastating news about his murder. He didn't feel it was his place to tell her since he really didn't know her well enough to be the bearer of bad news. His only other recourse was to return her to the hotel from where Maaches had kidnapped her. Jamaal met him in the study.

"Glad you're here." He took a piece of paper from the printer and handed it to him.

"What's this?"

"Read."

"The reward has been raised to one-hundred thousand dollars for the safe return of heiress Bethany Dailet. Her brother Shedrick and her uncle have been frantically searching for the archeologist professor since she disappeared a little over a week ago while standing outside a hotel in Cairo, Egypt, where she was attending a party. Bethany was a professor at the University of Indianapolis where she taught Ancient Cultures and History. She is engaged to realtor Mark Kauffman. Mr. Kauffman couldn't be reached for comment at press time." He stopped reading. "Engaged?"

Jamaal sighed. "How come that's the only word that registered in your head?"

Al scowled at him. "Because I knew everything else."

Jamaal folded his arms in front of him. "So why should you care?"

"I don't. She just never mentioned that she was engaged."

"You had one short conversation with her before you tossed her into the harem. That's not enough time to strike up a friendly relationship with her where she tells you all about her life."

"I'm not interested in her life, just the engaged part. What type of man would allow his fiancée to travel to a strange and distant country with a group of men?"

"The trusting type," Jamaal answered.

Al shook his head. "No, only the stupid or the neglectful type."

Mark paid the taxi driver and carried the baggage to the front door of the Royal Luxor hotel. The entire trip had cost him a tidy fortune…almost all the money he had and he had to pawn a couple of treasured mementoes left to him by his grandfather to have enough money to buy decent luggage and clothes. He didn't tell anyone except Shedrick Dailet about where he was going and the young man stupidly agreed to give him enough money to live off for a couple of months. Bethany's older brother was a flamboyant playboy who spent most of his time abroad. He didn't really have a job of his own, but lived quite well off his father's money and the money of any rich young socialite he happened to be dating at the time. Ernest, being sane, made the responsible Bethany executrix of his estate, which meant she was in control of the vast fortune.

After checking in at the reservation desk, Mark went up to his room and unpacked. He didn't know how long he was going to be in Egypt, but long enough for the heat to calm down on Ernest's murder, or until he could figure out how to claim the one-hundred thousand dollar reward for Bethany. He loosened his tie, and then turned on the television set in his room, hoping to find an American station. There was one world news station and it would have to do.

"That's George Eisemann," he said, turning up the volume. "What's he doing on television?" He listened until the report ended. "Well, I'll be damned. Those lucky bastards have found an ancient tomb. They are going to be rich."

He found a piece of paper and pen and jotted down the location in Luxor where the rest of Bethany's group was staying. "How hard is it going to be to find them? There can't be that many Americans in Luxor."

He sat down in a chair wondering what kinds of things he could do to entertain himself while he was there. There had to be some kind of night life and he could use a drink. His plan was to take a nap and go out to see a little of the town later. Hell, he might even do a couple of tourist things to pass the time away until he found someone to tell him what he wanted to know.

CHAPTER 7

*B*ethany wandered back to her room. It was late and she was tired. Had she been alone she would have been trying to find a door, but Jabari walked a couple of steps behind her to make sure she didn't try anything funny. There was a very loud unmistakable moan filtering out from the room next to hers. Then there was a very feminine giggle. "What the hell is that?"

"Playtime," Jabari answered. "Someone is making love."

"Yuck."

"What's yuck? It's a perfectly natural act."

She opened her bedroom door. "I know that, but they don't have to be so loud about it."

Jabari chuckled. "That means it feels good. Good night, Ms. Bethany."

Bethany stepped further into the room and closed the door, listening while Jabari locked the door securely with his key. She removed her clothes and slid into bed. Her muscles ached from moving furniture and dusting all day.

"Ah, ah, oh, ooh."

"Perverts," Bethany muttered as the lovemaking grew louder. The only thing that separated the two rooms was a nearly transparent wall. The room next to her belonged to Lotus, so it was apparent she had been the lucky one chosen to be serviced by Al-Shar Khan.

"Shush. Someone will hear you," another feminine voice said.

Now that piqued her curiosity. *Two women. Al-Shar must be very pleased with himself.* Bethany listened but did not hear his deep voice.

"Remove the gown so I can see you better." It sounded like Eboni. "Let me see those beautiful breasts." It was Eboni and she was saying some very hot things.

"Not so loud or we'll wake Bethany." The two women giggled and then the sound muffled.

Bethany turned on her side toward the wall. Eboni's statuesque form appeared. She could barely make out the young woman's curves since the room was dark and the curtains were drawn. Bethany strained to see but the shadow disappeared from view. There was a humming sound. Bethany blushed. One of them was using a vibrator. A couple more grunts and then a cry of satisfaction. Someone was using a vibrator with a lot of expertise. Then there was silence.

Bethany flipped over on her back very confused and very aroused. She wasn't a lesbian so she never quite understood how two women could sexually satisfy each other. She sighed. It was understandable though. The women were virtually prisoners and the only men they ever saw were Kesi and Jabari, and they weren't really men anymore since they were eunuchs. And how often did they get to spend the night with Al-Shar? He was just one man and even he had his limits.

She had dated Mark for several years and had been intimate with him twice. Neither of them seemed to enjoy the experience. Both times he was able to reach an orgasm, but she had been left sexually frustrated. He kept promising to get better the next time, but the next time never occurred. In a way, she was glad that he had broken off the engagement. She couldn't see herself tied down to a man who couldn't perform adequately in bed.

Her chance to escape came the very next day. Bethany had earned the time out of the harem, and her eyes were on the gate the moment she stepped outside. There weren't very many guards late in the afternoon she noted as she and the other girls walked about talking. Eboni and Lotus talked on and on about some exhibit they wanted to visit in Cairo, while she tried to count the times the gates of the compound opened and closed.

"Al-Shar must be entertaining," Eboni said. "This might not be such a boring night after all."

"What do you mean by that?"

"Sometimes he invites us to the party to entertain."

"Entertain?"

Lotus nodded. "Dance and have drinks with his guests."

"Do you have to do anything else?"

"Sometimes, if you mean sex. But not if we don't want to. Al-Shar never forces us."

So, he was a pimp too. That figures.

"Maybe you'll get lucky and be asked to join us," Eboni said excitedly. "You're going to love it. There's always a lot of food and good music."

Not no way or no how. "I can't dance," Bethany lied. In fact, she was an excellent dancer. Her mother had sent her to dancing school when she was five and she continued her classes until she was eighteen. At one time, she even considered dancing as a profession until she took her first archeology class.

"We'll teach you," Eboni said. "It's easy."

Bethany's very keen eyes picked up on an unguarded section of wall. It was hidden away from the light by a bunch of trees. She made an excuse to get away from Eboni and Lotus and then tried to inch her way over.

Jabari and Kesi were busy flirting with a couple of guards and not paying any attention. Perfect. She slipped past a couple of women who were in the garden holding hands and kissing. *I've got to get out of here.* She made it to the trees, scaled the wall, and landed on her feet.

"What do you mean you can't find her?" Al screamed at Jabari. "When was the last time you saw her?"

"About two hours ago," Jabari confessed. "She was out in the yard with the rest of the women. I noticed that she was gone when it was time to escort the women inside."

"Where is Eboni? She was supposed to be keeping an eye on her."

"She's in her room. She hasn't seen her either. She thought she might have gone inside to use the bathroom."

"Well, did you check in there? Women spend a lot of time in the tub."

"Yes, I did, but she's not there. I checked her room, but it's empty."

"So you're telling me that the guards just let her walk right by them?"

Jabari shook his bald head. "Impossible. Kesi and I were talking with them the entire while. She never came that way."

"Which means that she scaled the wall at a place that wasn't guarded and got away?" He rose.

"What are you going to do?"

"I'll find her. She couldn't have gotten that far away. It's dark and I doubt if she knows her way back to town. Have Jamaal see to the guests."

Jabari nodded, stepping back to let Al-Shar pass.

Al hurried out the back door and headed toward the stables. He saddled up his horse and raced toward the gate. The guard had it opened and waiting for him. Scanning the area from all directions was no help. His place was located near the desert and was on a lone stretch of land. It was still unbearably hot and not safe for a woman to be out wandering around. He rode off in a northerly direction. He was about to give up after about an hour when he spotted her. "Damn fool woman," he muttered as he rode up on her.

Bethany heard him, looked around, and started to run. *She's fast but not faster than my horse.* He toyed with her for several minutes, letting her think she had the upper hand. "There is no place for you to run, my sweet," he said as he rode closer.

"Leave me alone," she shouted back angrily. "I want to go home."

"I thought I made it perfectly clear that I can't do that, especially since now there is a reward posted for you."

"I would think that would be proper incentive for you to take me back. How much is it?" She stomped away from him.

"One hundred thousand dollars. Someone really wants you back badly."

"I do have family, you know. My father must be going crazy wondering where I am."

No, he isn't. "And a brother and a fiancé."

Bethany stopped and looked up at him. "How do you know that?"

"I did my homework. Remember, I thought you were a spy."

"I could still very well be."

Al laughed. "No, you're an archeologist and you've just discovered what might the best archeological find of the century."

"You know about that too?"

"It's all over the news. Too bad you're missing out on all of it."

"You're a bastard."

"Yeah, I know." He picked her up on the horse so fast she didn't have time to protest. "So tell me about this fiancé of yours." He turned the horse and headed back home.

The heat of his body next to hers as they rode back made her dizzy. She had to rest her head against his muscular chest because she didn't have anywhere else to put it. He held her close to him, quite possessively. A notably sizeable penis rested between their bodies. So maybe the eunuchs weren't exaggerating, she mused. She only wished she could see the rest of his face. *I swear I think he has about a thousand masks in every color.* He was a brown-eyed oddity with a deep sexy voice. The rest of him just had to match. "Nothing to tell. He's a realtor."

"And a fool," Al retorted. "There is no way I would ever allow you to go to a foreign county."

"Allowed? I'm a grown woman. Mark does not own me."

"So he was perfectly okay with you going off with three men unchaperoned?"

"Sure he was. One of the men is old enough to be my father. One is a like a brother and one is…" *What category does Nicholas fit in?* "And one is a very good friend."

"The one with the computer? Yes, I remember him. He was the one hovering over you that day you fell down that hole."

Geez, was there anything he didn't know about her? "Yes. He and I were students together under professor Eisemann."

"For a moment I thought you were going to say that you were lovers."

Bethany stiffened against him. "No."

"But he wants to be?"

"Why so many questions?"

"Because I'm interested. There are not too many women I know who can scale a wall."

"Well, I grew up with an older brother. I hung around with him a lot when my father was away on digs. Climbing walls and trees just **comes** naturally."

He tightened his grip on her as he turned the horse again. The move sent her body sliding snuggly between his legs. His erection was thicker than before. She smiled smugly. It serves him right. "So, what about you? Why are you a bandit?"

He chuckled. "For numerous reasons, all of which are just hyped by the media. They made me a bandit by assumption. I cannot help their perception of me."

"You're always masked. And weren't you running from the police that day we met?"

"A misunderstanding. I just happened to be in the wrong place at the wrong time."

"It doesn't explain the masks."

"For the dust."

"Ah, come on. I might be a bit naïve, but even I don't believe that. What are you hiding, Al-Shar?"

"My past," he replied. "I can help more people if no one knows my true identify."

"Help more people?"

"I was distributing food to some poor families who live in the cemeteries," he explained. "No one knows they're there except for me and a couple of others."

"Why are they living in the cemeteries?"

"Because they're poor and they have nowhere else to go. They are safe and off the streets."

"You're losing me here. So, the police were after you because you were delivering food to poor people who live in the cemeteries?"

"Yes, that's exactly what happened. They assumed that we were looting the place. We rode off quickly because we didn't want them to discover the people there."

The explanation was plausible enough, but she didn't believe him. They turned another bend.

"So where were you going?"

"Back to the hotel."

"You do realize that you were headed in the wrong direction?"

"Gee thanks."

"Is it so bad being here with me?"

"Last night I heard two women making love very loudly. What do you think?"

Al laughed. "Is that all? I suppose they don't have lesbians in the United States?"

"Yes, they have them, but I don't happen to sleep in a room next to them."

"So what's wrong with a little harmless sex between friends?"

"That's what you are there for, isn't it? Aren't you supposed to service them?"

"Technically yes, but physically, no."

"That's not what I've heard. I heard you know how to please a woman and sweep her off her feet with your kisses."

Al chuckled. "All lies."

Boy I certainly hope not. If his kisses did half of what his voice is doing to me then I might certainly consider a life of crime.

They arrived back at his home. The guards opened the gates for them. Al climbed off the horse first and then helped her down. "Are you going to run away again tonight?" He held her up in his arms with her pressed tightly against him. He buried his face into the crook of her neck. Her breasts instantly responded to the feel of his lips against her skin. Bethany pushed him away and he allowed her to slide down to the ground.

"No, I won't be running again tonight, nor doing anything else."

He opened the door and allowed her to enter first. He followed. "Anything else is the furthest thing from my mind."

She tossed her hair saucily. It was one lie she did believe. Jabari was waiting outside her door. "Lock me in," she told him. "Nice and tight."

Al laughed and went back to his guests.

CHAPTER 8

"It's been a week. Do you think we're going to find her?" Nicholas asked George as they prepared to go back to the bungalow after being at the dig all day.

"Yes. I have faith that they will find her soon."

Nicholas hoped he was right. He didn't know how much he missed her until she wasn't there. He had been in love with her since the first day he saw her walking across the campus of the university. Even back then she was pretty with her long blonde hair, baby blue eyes and smile that could light up the sun. Add brains and a wonderful personality and you had the perfect woman. Being shy kept him from ever asking her out on a date. By the time he had found the nerve she was dating Mark Kauffman. They announced their engagement before she graduated from college.

For the next couple of years Nicholas continued to worship Bethany from afar until his dreams came true and she saw Mark for what he really was…a lying, scheming son of a bitch.

"You'll see. She'll be here just in time for us to open the doors of the tomb. She wouldn't miss that opportunity for anything." They got into the SUV and drove back to the bungalow.

He knew something was up the moment he saw the strange rental car parked just outside the gates. His heart nearly dropped to his feet when they walked in and found Mark Kauffman sitting in the living room waiting for them.

"What the hell are you doing here?"

Mark rose. "Now is that any way to greet the fiancé of the woman you're in love with?"

"The two of you are no longer engaged."

"I didn't hear you deny the last part."

"You're a bastard."

Mark laughed and then turned his attention to George. "Have you heard anything yet?"

George entered with Andre close on his heels. He took off his hat and sat down. "Nothing yet. The police have questioned a few suspects but they haven't come up with anything tangible."

"Can you at least tell me what happened?"

"All we know is that two masked men snatched her from in front of a hotel. She had just stepped outside."

"And you let her go out alone?"

"She insisted," Nicholas replied. "She was just going out to warm up a bit because the room we were in was cold. I offered to go with her but she refused."

Mark turned on him. "So, it was your fault." He braced up to Nicholas who was taller by at least a foot.

Andre stepped between them. "No, it wasn't and you didn't answer the question. Why are you here?"

Mark pulled away and brushed off his jacket. "I came here to look for her. What do you think?"

That he knows about Ernest's death and that he is hoping to get his hands on some of the inheritance money. Nicholas frowned at the money-grubbing bastard. "What do you think you can do that we haven't done already?"

"I don't know. All I know is that I just couldn't sit around Indianapolis not knowing if she was dead or alive. Someone has to know something. I'll find her even if I have to search the entire African continent for her."

Nicholas rolled his eyes. He didn't believe one word of Kauffman's false confession of love. The only thing Mark cared about was himself.

~

"When are you planning to take her back?" Jamaal asked Al as they sat around the storage room putting together more care packages to deliver.

"In a couple of days. After I visit Emir Hatem."

"Why then?"

"Because I plan to take her with me and then drop her off on the way back."

"Any particular reason why you're taking her all the way to Mauritania?"

"Because she will just try to get away again if I leave her here until I return."

"Why not drop her off first and then go where you have to go?"

Al frowned at the inquisition. "Why not say what you want to say."

Jamaal folded his arms around his chest. "I think you're getting in way over your head. You're falling for this woman."

"So, what's wrong with that?"

"You know what's wrong with it. She thinks you're a thief for one, and you're holding her hostage."

Leave it to him to be sensible. That was probably why they had been friends all this time. "I promise to drop her off as soon as I return from Mauritania."

"What if someone recognizes her?"

"I'm way ahead of you. Eboni will take care of that. She'll put her in disguise."

"I guess I can't talk you into changing your mind."

"No.

Jamaal bowed and left.

"Why aren't we going out to join the rest of the girls for our walk?" Bethany asked Eboni after they had finished their chores. "Am I being punished for trying to run away yesterday?"

"No. In fact, Al-Shar is about to take you somewhere."

Bethany didn't like the sound of that. "Where? He didn't mention anything to me yesterday."

"To Mauritania. To visit with an old friend of his."

"He's not taking me there to sell me, is he?"

Eboni chuckled. "No, I'm afraid not. Al-Shar does not sell women...just horses."

"Why do all of you speak so highly of him? You're being held here against your will."

"No, we're not. Al-Shar took us in because we had nowhere else to go. We have no families."

"Huh?"

"We would be on the streets probably forced into prostitution. Al-Shar took us all in and all he asks in return is that we help take care of the place."

"You mean you're free to walk out of here any time you choose?"

Eboni nodded. "But we chose to stay."

Okay, maybe I'm wrong, or maybe Eboni is brainwashed. Either way I don't have time to worry about all that. My biggest concern now is why Al-Shar has decided to take me away. Maybe the police finally found out that he is holding me here.

Eboni's voice broke her thought. "We'll start with the hair. How do you feel about being a brunette?"

"I've never really thought about it considering I have always been a blonde."

Eboni pulled out a bottle of dye. "It's only temporary," she replied before Bethany could protest. "It will wash out after a couple of shampoos."

Bethany smirked. Al-Shar has it all planned, right down to the last detail. She thought about refusing to go along with his scheme, but she couldn't help but wonder what it would be like just to be alone with him.

There was a knock at the door several hours later. It was Kesi. "Al-Shar is waiting," he announced. "Is she ready?"

Eboni opened the door wider. "See for yourself."

Kesi gasped. "I hardly recognize her."

Bethany turned around and looked at her reflection again in the mirror. "I barely recognize myself."

Kesi held out his hand to her. "Come, Al-Shar waits." He led her through the house. Al-Shar stood next to the finest horse she ever laid eyes on. This one was midnight black with a spot of white on its snout. Like the horse, Al-Shar was all dolled up in black, except for the gold coils around his keffiyeh. He also wore a gold sash around his waist. The tunic had been replaced by a long-sleeved black shirt, open at the collar. Her eyes dipped down to pants that hugged his hips and legs like a glove. She, like he and the horse was also dressed in black. Eboni had not only changed her hair, but bronzed her up with enough makeup to give her an exotic look. She accepted his outstretched hand and he pulled her to his chest. "I almost didn't recognize you."

"It's me." She tugged at the low neckline of the blouse. "And there's a whole lot of me showing that's not usually exposed."

"I'm digging the cleavage."

Bethany smirked. He knew more about American slang than he led her to believe. She removed herself from his grasp. "What's with the Zorro getup?" she asked as his eyes perused her every curve.

"We need to blend in with the night. We have a long journey ahead of us and we don't want to cause a distraction along the way."

She guessed that was a code for people were still searching for her. He helped her mount the mighty Arabian stallion. "This is a beautiful horse."

"Midnight is one of my favorites. He's just like a puppy." He climbed up in front of her and she wove her arms around his waist. Waving to Kesi and Eboni, Al-Shar urged the horse into a gallop.

The gates opened and they dashed off into the night. They rode for a couple of hours through the desert with only the moonlight to guide them. The heat was not as unbearable since the sun had gone down, and there was a miraculous breeze. There was something romantic about the desert at night, and she probably would have appreciated it more had she not been with a thief. Al-Shar slowed the horse to a pace. Bethany looked from behind him into the desert night.

She saw people, camels and wagons up ahead. "What's that?"

"A caravan of Bedouin." He turned the horse for her to get a better look.

It was an amazing sight. Bedouin travelers moved slowly on camelback, accompanied by lambs and sheep and men on horseback. One headed in their direction. Bethany tightened her hold around his waist.

"I appreciate the cuddling, but there's nothing to be afraid of. This is the caravan of my friend Basil Fawzi and his family."

The rider approached cautiously at first. Then apparently, he recognized either Al-Shar or the horse. His was dressed in an off-white Burnoose. His head was fully visible exposing wave after wave of deep brown hair. His eyes were also brown and soulful with a depth of ancient knowledge which she took as wise beyond his years. His beard and mustache was sprinkled with gray, which added to his rugged good looks.

He dismounted and walked over to them. "Welcome Al-Shar to the caravan of Fawzi."

Al-Shar slid from the horse and shook the man's hand. "Thank you, Basil. We have been riding several hours and need to rest." Basil signaled the caravan to come to a halt. Several men quickly went to work on erecting a huge tent before her feet were on the ground. "This is Bethany."

Basil stepped forward to greet her. "It is a pleasure. Please join me and my family. I want you to meet my people." He held her hand in his just a tad bit long for comfort, but pulling away would probably be an insult. She just smiled politely. "Where are you from?" he asked.

"The United States."

"That would explain your perfect command of the English language." He grabbed the reins of the horse and started walking toward the big tent, while still holding her hand. Al-Shar brought up the rear. "So, Bethany, what brings you to Egypt?"

"I'm here with friends. We've come to see the ancient tombs."

"A splendid reason, but don't forget that Egypt holds many other wonders. Leave the tombs to the dead." They walked a couple of steps. "How did you meet Al-Shar?"

"We met at a bazaar where he literally knocked me off my feet."

Basil laughed. "Why do I feel that she's telling the truth?"

"Because she is. I nearly ran her over when J. W. and I were fleeing the police."

"How is little brother?"

"Still being a pain. He was quite upset about my taking the shortcut. What could I do, the police were hot on our behinds?"

"Al, how many times have I told you to stay to the shadows? You will get more work down in the cloak of darkness."

J. W.? So that was the name of the other man. She had seen him lurking around Al-Shar's back a couple of times, but she couldn't see his face clearly. Basil called him little brother. Was he Al-Shar's brother or Basil's?

"Then I would never have met Bethany."

Basil chuckled. "That is what has kept us friends all of these years Bethany. Al-Shar never fails to be entertaining." He led them inside his tent which was already bursting at the seams with beautiful women and broods of children. They were plainly dressed and unadorned in traditional abayas decorated in hand-sewn embroidery. She didn't fail to notice that a couple of them smiled at Al-Shar, and one had the audacity to wink like she was much more to him than just a friend.

"That is my youngest sister Falaya," Basil explained when he felt her tense up next to him. "She has the eye for Al."

"All the women in Egypt seem to," Bethany replied as she settled down on a large pillow. "It must be the mask."

Basil sat down next to her. "Does it bother you?"

"Yes, even though I know it makes him, him."

"I like this one. She is intelligent and beautiful."

Al settled down on a pillow. "She has her moments."

Bethany rolled her eyes at him. "How long have the two of you been friends?"

"Since we were kids," Basil answered.

"Then you know what he looks like without the mask."

Basil accepted the bowl of meze, a dip made of tahini, chickpeas, garlic, lemon and mashed eggplant, and a basket of pita bread, from Falaya. He dipped a piece of the pita in it and then passed the food to Bethany. "Yes," he finally answered.

"And you're not going to tell me if the voice matches the face?"

Al-Shar chuckled. "Does it matter?"

She dipped her bread into the mixture and sampled it. "This is delicious." She chewed and passed the bowl to Al-Shar. She swallowed. "I'm just curious."

"She likes your voice," Basil said to Al-Shar. "That is a good sign."

Al dug into the dip. "Don't let that beautiful face fool you. Behind those big blue eyes is a very conniving mind. Last night she got away from Kesi and Jabari by scaling the wall of the compound."

Basil laughed. "What did you do? This is the first time I've ever heard of a woman running away from you."

CHAPTER 9

Their short stay with Basil and his people ended early the next morning. They said goodbye to their generous host and rode off into the sunrise. Al slowed the horse down to a gentle trot. "When are you going to tell me where you're taking me?"

"Why didn't you ask me that earlier?"

"Well?"

"Well, we are going to see another old friend, Emir Abdul-Malik Hatem, and his family. He has invited me to a party."

"You're friends with an Emir?"

"You sound surprised."

"A little. So is it much further?"

"Sick of sand already?"

"A little. I could use a nice long bubble bath."

Al conjured the picture up in his mind and shuddered. "Do you like to take bubble baths often?"

"Every chance I get. One of these days when I own my own home I'm planning to have a big sunken tub put in."

"You don't have your own home?"

"No, I live with my father. I was planning to move out after I graduated from college but he became ill."

"That is very commendable of you. Most kids would have just moved away and gone on with their lives."

"Do you have any family?"

"Yes. Both of my parents are still alive, and are about to celebrate their fortieth wedding anniversary. And I have a sister."

"And do they know what you do for a living?"

Al chuckled. "Yes, curious Bethany."

"And do they approve?"

"I'm thirty-years old. What can they say?" He paused as he saw something out of the corner of his eye. "Oh, oh."

Bethany gripped him tightly around the waist. "What's wrong?"

"I don't have time to explain. Just hold on tight."

Before she could ask why, he put the horse into a full speed gallop toward a clump of trees. Seconds later, he snatched her from the horse, and pulled the horse behind them. The wind whistled around them.

"What is that? Why do I hear wind in the desert?"

"Dust storm," he shouted above the gale.

The winds picked up before he had a chance to continue and it whirled and spread out all around them. He grabbed the pack from the back of the horse, pulled out a tent and quickly erected it on the spot. He pushed Bethany in and crawled in behind her.

"What about the horse?"

He zipped up the tent and pulled Bethany to him. "He will be okay."

"How long is this going to last?"

"Long enough. I just hope the tent survives."

"I've heard of that occurring but I've never witnessed it."

"Every now and then one appears in the desert. Sometimes with devastating effects."

Bethany trembled next to him. "It's going to be all right. Just close your eyes." Sand hit the tent, rattling it.

"It sounds like a tornado."

"It is, just without the rain." He kissed her on the forehead. "It should be over soon." Minutes later the wind died down and it was calm. Al waited for a moment, enjoying the feel of her in his arms. They had just one more night together and then it would all be over. He released her.

"Do you think it's safe to go out? What if it starts up again?"

"We'll never know unless I check." He unzipped the tent and peeped outside. Midnight whinnied. The horse had survived. He crawled out and looked around. Bethany followed him out.

"Why does it look different around here?"

"Nature has a way of changing the scenery with things like dust storms to break up the monotony." He rose and pulled Bethany to her feet. Midnight whinnied again. Bethany ran over and hugged the horse. "Hey, what about me?"

"You were safe inside the tent."

Al marched over and took down the tent. "Damn lucky horse." He shook away the sand, refolded it, and packed it away again. "Come on. We still have a long way to go before nightfall."

"Where are we?" Bethany asked as she stared down on what looked like a small palace. It was constructed of pristine white brick with tall squared top columns at each corner. Numerous rectangular windows gave the place an open feel. Bright lights from inside made it visible in the dark. A red, green, and white flag flapped slowly in the warm breeze from a pole atop the white domed roof. Two large palm trees had been planted at each side of the entrance for landscaping. It was breathtakingly beautiful, but what caught her attention was the lake on the right side of the palace. It was the last thing she expected to see in the desert.

"We have arrived at our destination." He pointed down into the canyon. "And that is the palace of Emir Hatem." Al chuckled at her wide-eyed expression. "You act like you've never seen one before."

"Only in books." He helped her back on the horse. "How are we going to get way down there?"

Al jumped on ahead of her. "We are going to ride."

Bethany closed her eyes as they went down into the steep canyon, praying that they wouldn't fall. She opened her eyes just in time to see a group of turban wearing men heading in their direction.

"Emir Hatem has sent his guards to greet us."

"Al-Shar," one of them shouted. "The Emir was worried about you. He thought you weren't coming."

"Now would I miss a party?" he asked the man when he neared. "We ran into a dust storm. Other than that, nothing can keep me from this place."

"Follow us. The festivities have already started."

Arabian music echoed through hills as they rode down. The guards escorted them to the gates and left them to venture in on their own. Al helped her down and a young boy arrived to take the horse off to the stable. Al led her up the stairs and through the doors, where her feet sank into thick Persian carpet, and her nostrils picked up the most tantalizing aromas. Her stomach growled loudly.

Al laughed. "We'll get rid of that in a moment but I have someone I'd like you to meet first."

He opened a set of doors and escorted her inside.

"Al-Shar," several women shouted as they entered. People fell to their knees and bowed as he walked by.

"Is this customary?"

"Yes," he replied. "I practically grew up in this place The Emir is like a father to me, so I am treated as such."

A thief, a humanitarian, a pimp, and now the son of an Emir. How many other personalities does he have? Children ran up and hugged his legs. Al scooped one of them up and hugged her tightly. She was about seven and all dressed up like a princess.

"Papa said you were coming. I can't wait to show you my new doll I got from Cairo." He put her down.

"And I can't wait to see it, Jasmin."

The little girl looked over at her. "Who is that?"

"Jasmin this is my friend, Bethany. Bethany this, is the Emir's youngest daughter, Jasmin."

"Nice to meet you, Jasmin?"

Jasmin looked her up and down with wise old eyes. "Are you a princess? You look like a princess."

"No, I'm not a princess."

"Then are you Al-Shar's girlfriend?"

Bethany blushed. "No, we're just friends."

"Papa said Al-Shar should get married."

Bethany laughed. Al-Shar did not. "Your papa has a big mouth."

An elderly man dressed in purple and gold satin appeared. On his head sat a turban with the biggest ruby Bethany had ever seen planted in the center. "Yes, I do," the Emir agreed. "And I mean everything that I say." He grabbed Al-Shar in a bear hug. "It's about time you got here. Mama has been asking for you, and Khalaf is already stoned." He freed Al. "And who is this desert flower?"

Al pushed her forward. "This is Bethany. I wanted her to meet you."

Abdul hugged her. "I'm honored. Al has never brought a woman home before." He winked. "Your mother will be so pleased. She is beautiful." He released her. "Come, you must be tired. Let me show you where you can freshen up." He clapped his hands and a girl appeared. "Take Al-Shar to his room and put Ms. Bethany in the room next to his. They have been on the road for days. See to their needs."

The young woman bowed. "Yes, sahib."

"I'll go and tell mama that you are here." The Emir hurried off in another direction. The young woman led them up the stairs and deposited Al-Shar at one door.

"I shall see you shortly," he said. "You're going to love this place."

The young woman whisked her off before she could respond.

Al found his way to the party after he showered and changed into suitable clothes. The Emir's wife, Nailah, squealed and nearly hugged him to death until Abdul wrestled him away. "Let the boy breathe." Al sat down and accepted the water pipe the Emir handed him.

He inhaled and let the smoke slip past his lips. "This is good stuff," he said once he exhaled.

"Only the best for you, Al-Shar. J. W. told me that you nearly got yourself caught by the police a couple of weeks ago."

Al nodded. "It was a close call, but we got away."

"It's a very noble thing that you do, but don't you think there's an easier way to do it?"

Al shrugged his shoulders. "Our people are proud. They will not accept the money if they knew who I was."

The Emir shook his head. "But to be in disguise. Your poor mother would be horrified if she knew the truth."

"She's not the one I'm worried about. My father would never understand."

Abdul waved the thought away. "Have you tried talking to him about it? I've known him for a long time. He's fair."

"No, I haven't. I'm not afraid, but he and I don't always see eye to eye on things."

"I think you need to tell him. Maybe he can help." He looked toward the stairs. "What about your friend. Does she know the real you?"

Al shook his head. "Not that she hasn't tried."

"Is she the one they're looking for?"

Al nodded. "Damn Maaches. He traded her to me for ten horses."

Abdul laughed. "And she's still with you?"

"Yeah. She was pissy mad at first, but she's calmed down some. I'm taking her back tomorrow."

"Why has it taken so long?"

"My fault. I just wanted to get to know her first."

"Perfectly understandable. I would never believe that you would lose your heart to an American woman."

Al lowered his head. "Me neither. It took me quite by surprise too. But it was never meant to be. I won't ever see her again after I drop her off in Luxor. It won't be safe and I'm not sure she won't turn me in."

"Are you sure she would do it?"

Al shrugged his shoulders again. "I don't know. But I can't take the chance. Too many people are depending on me."

Abdul inhaled from the pipe and then passed it back to Al. "Enjoy the night. You've earned the rest."

"Isn't this the woman we snatched from the hotel?" Sabola asked when he entered the bar. He pushed a newspaper toward Maaches.

Maaches looked down and then snatched the paper up so he could see it clearly. "Yes."

"Damn," Sabola replied angrily. "Look how much she is worth and we traded her for ten lousy horses."

Maaches read the entire article and then pushed the paper aside. "I bet

Al-Shar knew who she was the moment he saw her and intentionally kept her for himself."

"Do you think he's going to turn her in for the reward?"

Maaches nodded. "If he's smart he would. What is one woman when he has an entire harem at his disposal?"

Sabola sat down angrily. "I have half a mind to go and steal her away from him. We need the money more than he does."

Maaches rubbed his chin. "That doesn't sound like a bad idea, but we need a plan. We can't just go to his home and just steal her away. We would never get past the guards."

Sabola snapped his fingers after giving what Maaches said some thought. "I have it. Al-Shar likes to hang out in cemeteries. Why not snatch him, have him give us the girl and then turn him in for the kidnapping. We'll have the girl, the reward money and Al-Shar will be blamed for the entire kidnapping."

Maaches smiled. "You're a genius."

Sabola grinned. "I know."

It was a scene out of Aladdin. Bethany peered into the mirror after her bath. Arabian women of all ages crowded in the room with her offering advice on what to wear to dinner.

"The white one," Jasmin insisted. "It will go well with her skin."

"You're very perceptive for seven."

"Mama is teaching me."

"Then I'll wear the white."

One of the girls helped her into the outfit, which fitted her like a glove. The built-in bra pushed her breasts up so firmly that they spilled over the cup. "Ooh, I didn't know I had this much." The other women laughed.

"I told you that she was a princess," Jasmin replied. "Al-Shar is going to be so pleased."

Bethany didn't know how to react to her statement. "Where is he anyway?"

"He's downstairs with my brother and the other men. We will be joining them shortly for dinner."

Another woman entered with slippers for her, while one arranged her hair. Several minutes later Bethany walked down the stairs. She found Al-Shar and another very handsome man sprawled out on pillows being fed grapes by two women. Al had changed into a blue outfit similar to the one the other man wore, including the turban and a blue mask. Darn, she thought that he would relax enough to remove it. But that was not the current problem. The problem was the dark eyed vixen who was almost sitting in his lap. Jasmin dragged her into the room and then hurried off to join the rest of the children. Bethany cleared her throat to get his attention. Al looked up and nearly pushed the other woman off him. The young lady retreated to the other side of the room, dragging the other girl with her.

"Who is that beautiful enchantress?" Khalaf asked.

Al sat up and saw the look of surprise on Bethany's face. "That is Bethany, my date for the evening."

He got an elbow to the side. "So how come you haven't mentioned this one before?"

"Because we've just met and because I know how you are around beautiful women."

"You hurt my feelings, Al."

Al chuckled. "You'll get over it."

Bethany walked over to them, a vision in virginal white.

"Does she know who you really are?"

"No, and I want to keep it that way for now."

"Ah, that would explain the mask."

Bethany came to stand next to them. Al and Khalaf sprang to their feet. "Bethany, may I present Amizada Khalaf Hatem. He is Emir Hatem's oldest son." Khalaf took her outstretched hand, brought it to his lips and kissed it.

"Mighty nice to meet you," Bethany said breathlessly. "Al-Shar failed to inform me that the Emir had such a handsome son." Al frowned. Those weren't exactly the words he expected to come from her lips.

Khalaf took her hand and placed it in the crook of his arms and led her deeper into the room. Al followed. "That's because Al-Shar is very jealous and very selfish. He wishes to keep all the beautiful women to himself."

He led her over to some chairs and helped her into a seat. "How long have the two of you been friends?"

"Too long," Al answered for him, well aware of what Khalaf was trying to do. The two of them had been very competitive as kids.

"I have known him since infancy. We shared a crib a couple of times. Al was a trouble-maker and he always got us into trouble."

Bethany arched an eyebrow at him. Al looked away. "He hasn't changed much."

Khalaf laughed. Al protested. "I don't quite remember it that way."

Khalaf ignored him. "You wouldn't, but Bethany believes me. He was always sneaking girls into the palace and smoking."

Bethany laughed. "You've been corrupt since birth, a teen-aged juvenile delinquent, and now a bandit."

Al scowled at her. "I thought I made it perfectly clear that I'm not a bandit."

"Just because you say it isn't so doesn't make it so."

Khalaf belched loudly. "Finally, a woman who isn't swayed by smooth words."

Bethany giggled. "Ooh, I think I'm going to like you."

Khalaf laughed. "I think you will too."

Al continued to scowl as Khalaf danced Bethany around the floor. Abdul nudged him with his slippered foot. "Don't the two of them look good together?"

"No they don't."

Abdul laughed. "Ah, you're jealous."

Al pouted. "I am not."

"Sure you are. There is nothing like a little rivalry to get the juices going."

"There is nothing going on between Bethany and me. She is free to dance with any one she pleases."

"You're jealous. I can see it in your eyes."

Nailah popped her husband with a pillow. "Stop teasing the boy. Of course he's jealous. Khalaf is a very handsome man and he is a good dancer."

"She thinks I'm a bandit and a thief and she does not trust me."

"Have you given her any reason to? You hide yourself behind that mask like a common crook," Abdul replied.

"I have my reasons. Besides, it will all be over tomorrow."

"You first have to make it through the night." He laughed. "Personally, I don't think you're going to make it."

CHAPTER 10

*M*aybe he should have stopped Bethany from smoking the water pipe he reasoned as he watched her dash off with the other young women. He hoped none of them would slip up and tell her anything about him. Khalaf sat down next to him on the floor. "Here, this will ease the pain." He handed Al a huge water pipe.

Al inhaled and passed it back to him. He let the smoke trickle out slowly. "What pain?"

"Of finally losing a woman to me." Khalaf took a long drag from the pipe and passed it back to him.

Al accepted it and inhaled deeply. The hit went straight to his brain and fogged up his senses. "That will never happen, and besides Bethany is not my woman." He blew out the smoke. "Plus, she hates my guts." He inhaled on the pipe again and then passed it back. "Can you believe that?"

Khalaf inhaled. "Yes, I can. You can be most difficult at times." He exhaled. "This is some good stuff." A young woman passed and smiled at him.

"Who is that?" Al-Shar asked.

"That is Isis. She wants me desperately."

Al nearly choked from laughing. "It must be quite wonderful high up there on your pedestal."

Khalaf laughed and agreed. "Yes, it is. Being the son of an Emir does have its perks."

Music started to play. Al turned his attention to the door. The women had returned in their costumes and prepared to dance for them.

"The entertainment has arrived," Khalaf announced as he put the pipe down to watch. "Where is Bethany?"

Al shrugged his shoulders, distracted by all the smiles he was receiving from the dancers. He watched with interest as they swayed and rolled to the melodic Arabic song. Although he was an experienced dancer he had a fondness for the traditional cultural dances of his people. Belly dancing was still a popular form of exercise and these women were in excellent shape. The tempo picked up and the girls whirled and twirled and performed gymnastics while the audience cheered and clapped encouragement. The Emir and his wife had returned and joined him and Khalaf on the pillows. "Have you seen Bethany?" he asked Nailah.

"She's upstairs in her room. She'll be down shortly."

"You two look so wasted," Abdul replied.

Khalaf handed his father the pipe. "You need to catch up."

The music changed, the lights lowered and the dancers disappeared from the room. Moments later one woman entered and began to dance for them. She was dressed in a pink and gold harem costume made of veils and very little else. Her face was covered by a dark pink veil and she used a bigger pink one to hide behind. She danced slowly at first, rocking her hips so that they moved on their own. She turned around and her long dark pony-tail swayed down her back as she rolled her butt in a slow circle. Al gulped. She had the sexiest behind and legs he had ever seen. The tempo increased and she jumped, twirled and teased the audience into clapping. She spun around and tumbled, but did not unveil her face.

"Who is that?" Al asked Khalaf.

Khalaf shrugged his shoulders. "Possibly the future mother of my first child." He sighed. "Isn't she superb?" He sat up straight when the music changed and she removed one of the veils on the skirt. "I think this is about to get interesting." She tossed the veil to him. "Very interesting."

A second veil came away from the skimpy costume revealing a thigh. She tossed it at another man in the room.

Al sighed. "Just look at those legs."

"I can't," Khalaf confessed. "My eyes are glued on those spectacular breasts."

The woman removed the long trail of her costume and draped it around her upper body, using it as a prop to lure his eyes up to her bosom while she worked the third veil free. "Isn't this dance forbidden?" he asked.

"Not in my kingdom," Abdul replied. She rewarded him with the third veil. He giggled like a school boy. "Mama you have to learn how to do that for me."

The young woman finally tossed the trail and removed her veil.

Khalaf looked over at Al. "This is too much."

Al scowled. *What is that little minx up to?*

Bethany moved in his direction, swaying hips he never knew she possessed, and showing off way too much cleavage. Her eyes were glued to him as she danced. Slowly the fourth, fifth and sixth veil came off. The men clapped and urged her to remove the seventh veil. She shook her head and continued to tease them.

"I wonder what she's hiding under that seventh veil." Khalaf asked.

Al growled at him. "You're never going to find that out." His eyes followed the veil as it moved enticingly between her legs.

"You didn't tell me that she could dance."

"I didn't know either. She is an archeologist."

"Look at that body. She can explore me any time she wants to." He gulped. "It's funny what clothes will hide."

Bethany's hand went toward the veil, and before he knew it, he was up on his feet and stopped her before she exposed anything else to the inebriated crowd. "No more, little Salome. My heart can't take it."

He tossed her over one shoulder, ducking all the men who tried to get at the final veil.

"Let me down you brute," she squealed. "I am not a sack of potatoes."

He slapped her soundly on the rump, much to the delight of the audience and carried her over to their pillows. The music ended just as he pushed her down on her back and lowered his lips to hers. Al broke the kiss first and tugged her to her feet to join him on the dance floor. Bethany giggled, stumbled a little, and joined him in the fun and before he knew it everyone was dancing and having a good time. He knew he was in trouble the moment the music changed to a slow song. Bethany wrapped her arms tightly around his waist and laid her head against him. He smiled. He thought maybe both of them had had a little too much to smoke. She had begged him to sample it. He probably shouldn't have allowed it. Without it though, there was no way she would allow him to hold her this way. His own head was a bit foggy. Maybe he should give up the pipe as well.

"I think I'm high," Bethany confessed.

Al chuckled. "What was your first clue?"

"The belly dancing. I hope they don't run me out of the country for doing the forbidden dance."

"I don't think so. Anything else?"

She sighed. "Being in your arms like this." She giggled. "For all I know you might be plotting to sell me to Abdul or Khalaf."

He pulled her tighter to him, pressing his body into hers. "Do you feel that? He asked about the budding erection she was causing.

"Yes. It's very impressive."

"I'd rather kill than sell you."

"Does that mean that you desire me?"

"That's exactly what that means. That's why I stopped the removal of that seventh veil. I wanted to be to one to remove it."

Bethany chuckled. "You're higher than I thought. The next thing I know you'll be professing that you love me and saying that you want to marry me."

"All you have to do is say the words and it can be arranged."

"I think I need more of the herbs," Bethany replied. "Before I do it."

"Do what?"

"Marry you."

Al chuckled. "So you have to be stoned out of your head."

"No, just teasing. There isn't a Justice of the Peace here."

"The Emir can do it."

She laughed. "You're crazy. What was in that pipe? I think you've lost your mind."

They stumbled back to the pillows. "Don't you think it's about time that you change?"

"Yes, but I think I'm too stoned to walk."

He picked her up and carried her up the stairs, opened the door and tossed her on the bed. She tried to get up, but he blocked her way. "Why did you choose that particular dance?"

"I like to belly dance. It's fun."

"Is that what they call it these days? It looked like a strip-tease."

"I had fifteen years of dance classes," she replied. "I know how to work an audience. I wasn't going to remove the last veil."

Al snatched it from around her waist, exposing pink and gold panties. There wasn't much to them except a piece of cloth that barely covered her pubic area. He dropped to his knees and ran his hand over her thigh.

Bethany pushed his hand away. "I chose the dance because I wanted to tease you into loosening up. You looked like you were about to strangle Khalaf for dancing with me."

Al sat down on the bed. His head felt fuzzy. "Well, he was holding you too close."

"Well, you sound like you're jealous and we both know that couldn't be possible because you like your horse more than you like me."

She slid off the bed and stood over him. Al looked up. She had her hands on her hips, but she was a bit unstable on her feet. "Did you have anything to drink while you were with the women?"

"Nope, just the pipe. Why?"

"Because you seem to be drunk."

"Maybe so," she replied as she stepped over him. "But not drunk enough." He watched her strip out of her costume.

Al jumped to his feet. "Maybe I'd better leave." He turned and hurried out of the room before the bra hit the floor.

He found Khalaf involved in a conversation with the young woman who had smiled at him earlier. Khalaf sent the young woman off. She kissed him on the cheek and dashed upstairs.

"You didn't have to send her away," Al said.

"I'll catch up with her in a few minutes. She's gone up to warm my bed. Anyway. You seem like you need to talk. You look like you've seen a ghost."

Al sat down. "Not a ghost, but a pair of tiny pink and gold panties."

"Ah, the mystery behind the seventh veil."

Al nodded.

"So what are you doing back down here? Even the old folks are gone to their room for a bit of fun."

"Didn't I tell you earlier that she hates me?"

"That dance was for your benefit. I didn't see hate anywhere in it." He sighed. "And it gave me get an erection like you wouldn't believe."

Al smiled. "You never could take seeing a little flesh."

"Yeah, I think she had every man in the room on fire." He smiled. "Where is the little tease?"

"Up in her room changing into something decent."

"You're a bigger fool than I thought. You went upstairs with a half naked woman and you made her put on clothes?"

"As tempting as it was, I couldn't take advantage of her. She's high as a kite."

"You've changed," Khalaf said with a laugh. "The old you wouldn't have given it a second thought."

Khalaf looked down at Al's sleeping form as he cuddled a pillow next to the sleeping beauty Bethany in the parlor. He smiled, walked away, and headed toward his father who had come down for water. "You know Papa, sometimes I think that Al is too stupid for his own good and wouldn't know a good thing if it was staring him in the face."

Abdul laughed. "I know what you mean. It's obvious that he loves her, but he thinks he can't have her because he's keeping too many secrets. He should have listened to J. W. and took her back before it went this far."

"I know she loves him too," Khalaf agreed. "Did you see the look in her eyes when she danced for him?"

Abdul nodded. "She had me hot for her and I'm old enough to be her father." He chuckled. "So what do you want to do about them?"

"I think we need to teach my arrogant, pig-headed brother a lesson."

Abdul agreed. "And I know just the thing. I think it's high time for him to have a mate." He smiled.

"You wouldn't?"

"Why wouldn't I? I can do it up nice and legal since this is my kingdom."

Khalaf laughed. "Al is going to flip."

"Let him. It's a much better fate than being arrested for kidnapping and slave trading."

Khalaf nodded. "I'll go wake them."

Al woke up on the floor. It was close to two in the morning when he decided to go to his room. His head throbbed and his vision was slightly blurred. He turned the knob and entered. The room was dark. Funny, he thought he'd left a light on. He disrobed and crawled into the bed. Try as he might, sleep did not come as easy as he thought it would. He moved around to get comfortable. His knees brushed something soft and solid. He wasn't alone. Rising up on one elbow he peered over at a pair of feminine shoulders. He smiled. Maybe Khalaf had sent him up a little appetizer. He ran his fingers down her arm to gently wake her. She turned and snuggled against him. "Not the response I was expecting, but it is something." He rubbed her arm again. "Wake up little one. You'll get to sleep later."

The young woman raised her head. "You smell good," she murmured in her stupor. She wrapped her arms around his neck. He recognized her.

Al tried to free himself but she clung tightly to him.

"I could just eat you up."

"You are so high," he said to her.

She rubbed up against him. "And I'm horny."

He knew he had to free himself from her soft, perfumed body and high tail it out of the room.

"Do you take off the mask when you make love?" Bethany kissed his chest.

Al gulped. If he didn't get away from her soon he'd be in serious trouble. "Sometimes," he replied as he slid down on the sheets. He brushed the mask aside and kissed her deeply. The taste of herb was still on her breath, which excited him. He pushed his tongue between her lips and she playfully suckled on his lower lip. His hands roamed freely over her body as she held on to him, kissing him feverishly. He removed her hands from his neck and crawled off her. He could not do it to her even if he wanted to. It would be like forcing himself on her and she was too inebriated to understand.

She rose up on one elbow. "What's wrong? Don't you still want me?"

Perspiration beaded beneath the mask. "Oh yes, I desire you very much, but I can't take advantage of you. You are stoned."

She squinted at him. "I am not. I just have a light buzz."

"Honey, you don't know where you are and who you're with."

"I'm on a bed with Al-Shar Khan." She crawled over to the end of the bed and pulled him toward her. "Are you afraid of me?" She began to unbutton her blouse, exposing a flesh-colored demi-bra. Her ample cleavage rose and fell with each breath she took. She removed the blouse, exposing creamy shoulders. She took down her hair and shook it free. "Am I not desirable enough for the great and powerful Khan?"

He wondered how many times his soul would go to hell for what he was thinking? He snatched the bra with one tug and her breasts bounced and then held firm. He climbed back on the bed, pushed her gently on her back and captured one of the rose bud nipples in his mouth.

Bethany moaned. "I guess that is a 'Yes'."

He had gone too far to stop now. He didn't think he could even if he wanted to. He had to see her completely naked and he wanted her trembling beneath him. Al removed the rest of her clothes and tossed them on the floor. He removed his shirt and pants and climbed back on the bed, capturing her lips. Bethany's hand went south and she squeezed him through his briefs.

Al moaned.

His cock was in pure sexual agony, as it grew hard with each squeeze. He brushed her hand away, wiggled out of the briefs, and then moved her hand back down on him so he could feel the full impact of her touch. The palms of her hand and fingers were as soft as talc. "Um." If she didn't stop what she was doing he was going to prematurely explode. He gently brushed her hand away again and slowly moved his mouth away from the breast he was nursing at and ran his tongue beneath it to tickle a little beauty mole.

"That feels heavenly."

Al continued downward to show her what felt good. He raised her hips and removed the tiny pair of flesh-colored panties. He tossed them to the floor and then turned back to her. "Oh wow," he uttered. He had hit pay dirt. Bethany was shaven. He buried his head between her legs and inhaled. She smelt feminine. He parted her thighs and gently ran his tongue over the lips of her vagina. She giggled. He plunged his tongue inside of her. Bethany thrashed on the bed and gripped the sheets. He took that as a sign to continue. He nibbled on the delicate skin beneath her opening. Al worked the area, thumping it with his tongue forcefully in a pattern that sent her over the top.

"Ooh, Al, ooh."

He buried his tongue back inside of her to help her ride out the rapids that rushed through her.

"Oh, oh, oh."

Al raised his head triumphantly, but she could not see the smile on his face because it was hidden behind the mask.

The woman had the recovery skill of a pro. Bethany sat up and then moved around the bed like a tiger stalking its prey. Her hair drooped down her face, but her eyes peeped out like blue neon. "It's your turn, Mr. Bandit." She wrestled him over on his back and playfully grabbed his penis between both of her hands. She lowered her head and deep-throated him. "Um," she said once she wiggled her lips free. "You're delicious."

The little stunt nearly sent him over the side of the bed in shock. So the vixen has skills. He laid back and watched her head bob up and down on his knob, applying pressure to just the right spots with her lips and jaws. She came up for air about ten minutes later, which was smart because he was on the verge of blowing.

Al sat up and snatched her to him, burying his face at her throat. He nipped her on the neck. She still hadn't sobered up much, which put him at a quandary of what to do. She took the decision away from him by mounting him and sinking down on his shaft. The fact that she had already been deflowered saddened him. She was still tight though, and it had probably happened with the bastard that called himself her fiancé. Up until now he had forgotten about this Mark Kauffman, the man he was about to send her back to tomorrow. Well, fuck him, she was his tonight.

Al put his hands on both sides of her waist and moved her up and down until they had a comfortable rhythm. She was still damp and she took more of him in with each downward descent. And she was so warm and comforting that he lost himself in the moment and allowed her to ride him forcefully until she shuddered into her second orgasm.

"You're multi-orgasmic," he whispered. He gently slid her off him and onto her back so she could rest. Their bodies were covered in sweat and his adrenalin was soaring. He didn't know how much more she could take but he planned to make it an adventure she would never forget. "Wake up Bethany. We're not quite finished yet."

"I'm awake."

"I want to take you from behind."

"Ooh, kinky."

He smiled. She was so out of it. She flipped over on her stomach and just laid there. Granted she had one luscious behind, but no, he wanted her on her knees. He lifted her into position and moved in behind her. He escorted his very ready penis inside of her.

"Oh," she gasped as he worked his way inside her tender core. She shook her head to move her hair out of her eyes. Al reached out and wrapped it around his hand without missing a stroke. He gave it a gentle tug. Bethany's head went back and he pushed his hips forward and slipped deeper inside of her. She rocked her knees and moved her body to keep up with him. It felt amazing as he slid in and out of the wet tunnel. He tugged her hair again.

"I wish I could do this forever," Al said He released her hair and it sailed back across her face.

She shook it and it floated down her back in dark waves. "I would probably let you if you can keep it hard all the time."

"I think there's a medicine on the market for that." He noticed that she was moving faster now. She was also getting wetter and fighting hard not to come. Al withdrew to stop her. "I don't want you to pop just yet." He wanted to take her missionary fashion so he could come with her. He flipped her over on her back, raised her leg, and plowed into her. He moved her hips with his hands back and forth on his penis. The friction of rubbing her this way made his penis thrash. "Oh, sweet Bethany, are you ready for this."

She moved with him. "Yes."

He pulled out and slowly moved it back in. "Yes, what?"

"Yes, Al-Shar."

He pulled out again, but this time he slammed into her hard. "Yes, Al-Shar what?"

"Oh," she moaned loudly. "Yes, Al-Shar I'm ready for it."

He pulled out for a third time, but he did not enter. He just ran the head around the outside of her vagina. "Ask me nicely."

"Please, Al-Shar. Don't make me beg. I need you now."

Al spread her open with his fingers and drove into her as far as he could. Bethany exploded on impact. She raked his back with her nails. Al bit his lip as he came with a vengeance. She wrapped her legs around him and used her vagina to suck every drop of him in. "Oh shit," he uttered loud enough to wake the entire house. He felt like he had shot out the Nile River.

CHAPTER 11

*a*l sat up and the covers slipped down from his chest and landed in his lap. Someone moved on the bed beside him. He looked over. "Oh my. What have I done?" Bethany snored peacefully beside him with nothing on but a smile. "No, we didn't." He shook his head and it pounded. "How much did I have to smoke?" He tried to recall but all he got was fog. Too much, he guessed by the state of the bed. Bethany moved in her sleep again. *Can this be real? Damn what did Khalaf have in that pipe?* A gentle contented sigh escaped her lips. Hmm, maybe they had. He looked down at his lap. There was evidence everywhere.

He smirked; surprised that she had allowed things to get that far considering that she hated him. That could only mean that she was as drugged as he had been. He wasn't looking for excuses. It wasn't like he hadn't entertained the idea from the moment Maaches dropped her on the floor at his feet, but he kind of hoped he would remember at least some of it. He eased out of the bed, gathered his clothes, and walked toward the bathroom. He needed a shower, a fresh change of clothes and a cup of very strong coffee. Al peeped in at Bethany about a half hour later. She was still flat on her back and unconscious. He'd send one of the girls up later with some clothes and toiletries, but there was no way he was ready to face her. He quickly closed the door and went downstairs to the kitchen.

The last person he expected to be up and about was Khalaf.

"What are you doing here? And where is Bethany?"

"She's upstairs sleeping like a baby." He looked around. "Is that coffee I smell?"

Khalaf nodded. "I have one hell of a headache."

"Yeah, me too."

Khalaf got up, poured him a cup and refilled his own.

Al sipped and grimaced. "This tastes like chicory."

"It is. Guaranteed to wake the dead."

Al sipped again and the warm liquid flowed through his body. He put the cup down. "What the hell were we smoking last night?"

Khalaf winked. "A secret blend sent to me by Malik, guaranteed to take all your inhibitions away."

"That's no lie. I didn't know where I was when I woke up and then I discovered that I wasn't alone."

Khalaf laughed. "Oh no? Who was with you?"

"Bethany."

"Oh, I see. Did anything happen between the two of you?"

Al shrugged his shoulders. "Both of us were naked when I awakened, so I kind of think so. But I can't be sure."

"What do you mean you can't be sure? Don't you remember?"

"Bits and piece, and the bed and my jock were very messy like we had a good time."

Khalaf laughed loudly. "You're crazy."

"And I had the weirdest dream. I was at some kind of ceremony, and you and papa were there."

"I hope I never get that stoned that I don't remember having sex. How do you know if you satisfied her?"

"I'll have to ask her when she wakes. If she doesn't kill me then I will know that I did an adequate job of servicing her." He chuckled. "But all jokes aside, I'm in deep shit here. I have to take her back today. How can I just drop her off as if nothing happened? I don't think I'm an uncaring bastard."

"You are by reputation."

Al sipped his coffee. "Yeah, I know."

"So, don't drop her off. Take her back to your place."

"You know I can't do that. Maaches and Sabola kidnapped her from in front of that hotel in Luxor and traded her to me. I know I should have taken her back on the night she arrived, but I thought she was a spy for the police. Then it really blew my mind when I found out who she really was."

"She's going to be famous."

Al nodded. "And I don't want to be famous for being the man who held her hostage."

"So?"

"So, I've just slept with her."

"I know this is the wrong time to ask this, but did you use any protection?"

"I doubt it, since I don't remember having sex. I can't walk away. Hell, I don't want to walk away."

"Maybe you won't have to."

Al put his cup down. "What do you mean?"

"Don't get mad, but papa and I did something last night."

"Why did you start the sentence with don't get mad? What did two sand demons do?"

Khalaf told him.

"You did what? And it's legal?"

Khalaf nodded. "He's the Emir. It's all perfectly legal. Now she won't dare to turn you in."

He jumped to his feet. "She is going to kill me if she finds out."

"What do you mean, if she finds out?"

"I have no plans on telling her. I'm going to take her back to Luxor and disappear from her life like the crook she thinks I am."

Khalaf sighed. "I was right. You are too stupid for your own good. But I will respect your wishes and won't breathe a word of this to anyone."

Bethany screamed. "Why am I naked?" She hopped from the bed. Her clothes were in a mess on the floor, along with a very familiar black mask. "Al-Shar!" Bethany ran into the bathroom and looked into the mirror. Her entire body was covered with bruises and hickies. "It must have been so good. And I don't remember any of it." She turned on the shower, groaned and said, "I am going to kill him." She peeped back into the room. "Where is he anyway?" She climbed into the shower. Every muscle in her body hurt and she had a pounding headache. "That's what I get for smoking that pipe." She never did anything so daring in her life. She never even tried pot. She was clean and presentable when he returned. He was dressed in brown trousers, a tan, short sleeved shirt and a dark brown mask. She smirked. "I was right. You do have a mask to match every outfit that you own."

He nodded.

She'd dressed in a pair of navy blue pants and a light blue short-sleeved blouse that she found on the clean, made bed when she got out of the shower. Luckily, she had buttoned the blouse up to hide the marks before she exited the bathroom.

"I'm glad you're up and ready," he said. "It is almost time to leave."

He made no mention of the night before, and seriously she would have been truly embarrassed if he did since she didn't remember. "How long do I have? I need to thank our hosts and say goodbye to everyone."

"We leave in thirty minutes. We have a lot of ground to cover before it gets too hot. Our things are already packed and saddled on Midnight."

What was wrong with him? Where was that arrogant-tongued bandit from yesterday? Could it be possible that he had not enjoyed himself?

"I'll be down in a minute. I just have to use the restroom again since there aren't any in the desert."

He nodded and left. Five minutes later she followed him down.

"You must come visit us again," Nailah said as they sat at the table eating a breakfast of fruit, bread, and juice. "We never get to see much of Al-Shar any more since he got that fancy house of his."

Bethany did not commit herself. "I've had a very nice time, probably the best time I've had since I arrived in Egypt."

"It doesn't have to end. Al-Shar's parents are planning this big anniversary party in a couple of months. Maybe we'll see you there."

I doubt it. There's no way he's going to take me to meet his parents if he won't even show me his face. "Maybe."

Al entered carrying Jasmin. "Are you ready?"

Bethany nodded and rose.

"I want to go with you," Jasmin told him as she wiped the sleep from her eyes.

"Not this time, darling, but I promise I'll come get you and take you with me for a nice long visit." He put her down.

"You promise?"

"Yes, I promise. Haven't I've always kept my promises to you."

She smiled. "Yeah, you're the best." She scurried over to Bethany and hugged her. "Take care of him."

Bethany hugged her and kissed her on the cheek. "I will," she whispered." She walked toward Al. "Thanks for the lovely time and the hospitality."

"Anytime," Nailah said. "Don't be a stranger."

Khalaf entered the kitchen. He was dressed in white lounging pajamas, with his hair pulled back, exposing his handsome face. She walked over to him and bowed. "Your grace. It has been a pleasure."

He grabbed her for a hug. "Don't look so sad. I know you are going to miss me most of all."

Bethany giggled and pushed him away. "I shall count the days until I see you again." He slapped her soundly on the rump. "Go before I change my mind and keep you here to dance for me."

"Dance?"

"You don't remember? You entertained us with the most remarkable rendition of the dance of the seven veils."

"No."

"Oh, yes."

Bethany blushed. She didn't remember that either. "Do me a favor. Never give me that pipe again."

Khalaf laughed. "I'm afraid I can't do that. Then you'll never dance again for Al either."

She looked at Al-Shar. His eyes twinkled with merriment. "We'll talk about it later," he said. "We have to get going."

They said good-bye one last time and Al-Shar led her out of the palace. Midnight waited at the foot of the stairs. He helped her on. She couldn't help but notice that Al-Shar didn't make eye contact with her. Was he ashamed of their time together? Was she that bad in the sack? Al climbed up on the horse and directed Midnight through the palace gates. Bethany looked back one last time and sighed as they rode up the gigantic hill that had terrified her on the way down.

Bethany couldn't take the silence anymore. They had been riding about three hours and she was bored. "Did I do something wrong?"

"No," Al-Shar answered.

"Then why the silent treatment?"

"I have a lot of things on my mind."

"Oh," she said. She yawned. "I'm tired. Can we stop for a while?"

"Lay your head against my back and rest if you like, but we still have a long way to go."

"You're mean," she muttered, tightening her arms around his waist. She laid her head against his back. "Wake me when you feel like being civil." She closed her eyes and the horse's gently hoofs on the sand lulled her to sleep.

The bullets whizzing past her head was a sure indication that it was time to wake up. The scenery had changed and they were no longer in the desert. "Where are we and what's going on?"

"Near Luxor and someone wants us to stop," Al-Shar answered. "They have been following us for some time now."

"Luxor?"

"Yes, I'm taking you back to your hotel."

His back tensed. She lifted her head. They were near some unfamiliar mountains. He ushered the horse up, and they dismounted. Al-Shar walked over to the cliff and she followed him. She peered down. "It's two people," he replied.

"What do you think they want?" Bethany asked as she watched the two men dismount. She couldn't see them clearly.

"Probably you."

"Me, why me?"

"The kidnapping reward, or have you forgotten?"

"I had for a moment. What about you? They could be looking for you. You probably have a lot of enemies in your line of work."

Al-Shar went for his pack. "We don't have time to argue about this now." He pulled out two guns. "Can you shoot?"

Bethany took the gun and hefted it in her hand. She aimed it at him. "Yes."

"Good. Stop playing around. They are advancing up the mountain as we speak."

Bethany lowered the gun.

A trigger clicked behind them. Bethany and Al-Shar turned around slowly. "I thought you said there were only two of them?"

"Hello Bethany darling."

Al-Shar looked from the man to Bethany. "Do you know this man?"

"Sure she does. Let me introduce myself. My name is Mark Kauffman, and I'm her fiancé."

Al-Shar stared at the other man, unimpressed. He was tall, blonde and average looking. The only thing that did impress him was the fact that he was smart enough to sneak up on them. The other two men appeared. It was Sabola and Maaches. Why wasn't he surprised? Money always brought out the worse in people...even bandits.

"See, I told you we would find her," Maaches told Mark.

Mark nodded. "You don't act like you're glad to see me, Bethany." He walked over and took the gun out of her hand.

"I am and a bit surprised."

"Why? The entire world has been searching for you. It's like you disappeared off the face of the earth. Your family has been worried sick."

Al noticed that he did not mention her father.

He left Bethany's side and walked over to him. "So, you are the one who kidnapped her. I was told that you're a very dangerous fellow, and wanted by the police."

"I have my moments."

Mark put the gun in Al's face and cocked the trigger. He did not move or blink. "I could kill you for what you have put us through."

"Does she look harmed to you?"

Mark looked over at Bethany. "No, which is lucky for you. Although I'm digging the dark hair." He took the gun out of Al-Shar's hand, moved away, but kept the gun trained on him.

"When are we going to get the reward?" Sabola asked.

"As soon as I let her brother know that I found her."

Sabola smiled. "Do you hear that Maaches? We are going to be rich."

Maaches nodded. "I knew your plan was going to work."

"And what plan was that, Maaches?" Al asked.

"To track you down and turn you over to the authorities for kidnapping while we enjoy the reward money."

"But Al-Shar did not kidnap me, Maaches, you did."

Mark laughed. "Yes, aren't they clever? I'm sure they are sorry for that, and turning in Al-Shar Khan to the police is a way of showing that they have turned over a new leaf."

Al scowled. He hoped Mark was kidding or he was very foolish to think that Maaches and Sabola were going to change.

"So what now?" Bethany asked.

Mark turned to the other two criminals. "Tie him up and let's get out of these mountains."

Al pushed Maaches away when he tried to tie him up. Maaches stumbled and the gun flew out of his hands. Both men made a run for the gun, but Maaches got to it first. Al kicked him in the face, knocking him flat on his behind. Al grabbed the gun. "I'm afraid I can't allow you to take me to the police."

"You're outnumbered," Mark said. "And both Sabola and I are still armed.

Al raised the gun and pointed it. He cocked the trigger and released. The bullet sailed and knocked the gun out of Mark's hand without nicking him. Sabola made a move but Al was faster. He re-cocked and shot the gun out of Sabola's hand too. Both men stared at him like he was crazy. "As I was saying before, I cannot allow you to take me to the police. I'm going to allow the young woman to go back with you. I was on my way to Luxor to return her anyway. Now you have saved me the trip."

"What makes you think we won't come after you?" Mark asked.

Al whistled loudly. "Look up."

Mark and the others looked up. The high cliffs above them were littered with men, all pointing guns in their direction.

Maaches gasped.

"My people have you surrounded. The choice is up to you. You can be a living hero, or a dead fool."

"So, you're saying you're just going to let us walk out of here and take Bethany with us?" Mark asked.

"No, I'm going to allow you to walk out and take Bethany with you. As for the other two…" He pointed and whistled again. Several of his men walked from around the side of the cliff. "We'll take them with us. Tie them up and take them away," Al ordered.

The new arrivals wasted no time in subduing Maaches and Sabola and collecting the guns.

"How did you know that they were following us?" Bethany asked.

"There's not much I don't know about," Al answered. "I have people everywhere."

"I'm impressed. What's going to happen to them? Are you going to kill them?"

Al walked over to her and pulled her into his arms. Mark started to protest and then stopped. "Don't worry your pretty little head about them. You just go with the nice fiancé and take Cairo by storm." He lowered his head, swept the mask aside, and kissed her hungrily. He released her and pushed her toward Mark. "Take her back to her people and you better be good to her." He whistled and Midnight appeared. Al jumped on the horse. "It's been a pleasure, Salome." He pulled the flesh-colored panties from his pocket, raised them to his nose and sniffed. "I will treasure our time together for an eternity." He laughed and rode off into the mountains.

CHAPTER 12

"Can you give me a description of the kidnappers?" a police officer asked Bethany the morning after she and Mark arrived at the bungalow.

"Arabian and both in their mid-thirties. The one named Maaches is about six feet tall and weighs about two-hundred pounds. He has dark hair and brown eyes. The other Sabola is tall, thinner and doesn't speak much."

The officer lowered the pad. "Do you realize how many men on this continent fit those descriptions?"

Bethany shrugged her shoulders. "That's all I can say. They snatched me and held me in a dark bunker."

Mark leaned against the bar in the lounge listening. She had neglected to mention Al-Shar Khan and he wondered why. Was there something going on between the two of them as the bandit had alluded to with his panty demonstration? Or, was she just trying to get at him? "Why don't you tell them about the third suspect darling?"

"What third suspect?" the officer asked.

He walked over to her and stood behind her. "Don't be afraid. You're safe now and he can't hurt you." He rested his hand on her shoulder. "I think his name is El-Car or something like that."

"Do you mean Al-Shar Khan?"

"Yes, that's it. She was with him when I rescued her. He was holding her hostage in the mountains when I subdued him, and got her away."

"Ah Mark, that's not exactly what happened. Al-Shar was returning me to Luxor when you and those two men just happened to ride up. He did not kidnap me or hold me hostage. He rescued me from Maaches and Sabola."

Mark dug his fingers into her shoulders. "I think Ms. Dailet is confused."

Bethany slapped his hand away. "I am not confused. Mr. Khan did not kidnap me."

The officer appeared confused. "Then can you tell me how you got from being with the kidnappers to being with Mr. Khan?"

"They traded me for horses. Al-Shar was bringing me back and that when all hell broke loose."

"You've been missing for two weeks. Were you with Maaches and Sabola all that time?" Mark asked.

"Not exactly."

"What do you mean, not exactly? When did the trade take place between Al-Shar and those men?"

"I'm not sure. It could have been on the night I was snatched or the night after. Maaches drugged me, so I'm not sure."

"So you've been with Al-Shar for over a week?"

Bethany nodded.

"Why didn't he bring you back then?" the officer asked.

"I don't know."

"And where were you being held all this time. Did he have you locked up?"

"No, I was at his home."

"You know where he stays? Can you show me where it is?"

"No. Like I said, I was drugged when they brought me there, and I wasn't really paying attention when we left because it was night. All I know is that we traveled through a desert."

"Something sounds fishy about the story," Mark replied sarcastically. "Sounds like he took his sweet time getting you back. I think he was holding her there against her will officer."

The officer agreed. "Yes, it does. In my book that makes him guilty of bartering in slave trade."

Bethany gasped. "Wait, hold it. You have this all wrong. I was not a prisoner. Al-Shar was sweet and kind and tended to me while I recovered from whatever drug Maaches gave me. I stayed with him because I wanted to, not because I was forced to be with him."

Mark frowned. "So what are you trying to say that this man is your lover?"

Bethany replied, "What difference does it make, Mark?"

"It makes a big difference. You and I are engaged."

"We're not engaged. You broke up with me six months ago. You're so busy trying to blame things on an innocent man that you'll do anything to make yourself look good in the eyes of this officer. Explain to him what you were doing with Maaches and Sabola."

The police laughed. "Lady, Al-Shar may be a lot of things, but innocent he is not." He turned to Mark. "But she has posed an interesting question. What were you doing with those two men?"

"I just happened to run across them while I was out trying to gather some information on Ms. Dailet's disappearance. I met them in a bar, so I asked them if they knew anything and they told me that they would tell me for a price. I used the reward money as a way to get them to help me. I had no idea that they were the ones who actually kidnapped Ms. Dailet."

"Ah ha," Bethany replied. "Now I understand. Now you get to keep the reward for yourself. I don't think my father will pay you."

He put his hand back on her shoulder. "Oh, Bethany dear, you don't know do you? Your father is dead." Her felt her shoulders slump. "He died a couple of days after learning of your kidnapping."

The grand ballroom was alive with music and merriment. Yahi sat on his throne looking absolutely bored to death as the procession line of people came by to meet him and his family.

"You can at least pretend to be enjoying yourself," Jamaal whispered to him. "Look at all the beautiful women."

Yahi put on his best prince smile. "I'm not interested. I'm bored to death."

"Why? You're rich, handsome and one day you'll be king."

"And I'm a snazzy dresser."

"And you're vain."

A week had gone by and his life had slipped back to its old routine.

"What do you think about the new archeological find in Luxor?" a reporter asked the king.

"I think it is wonderful, but they haven't gotten in yet. I've heard they are having problems unsealing the doors."

"It is rumored that the tomb might contain your ancestor, the pharaoh Amasis. If so, what are your plans to commemorate this incredible find?"

"Have a celebration of course. I find archeology exciting. I plan to invite the archeologists here to meet them."

"Thank you, your majesty," the reporter said. He went off to join the other reporters.

Jamaal nudged Yahi in the side. "I guess that piqued your interests."

"I don't know what you mean."

Jamaal chuckled. "You are such a liar."

"Maybe we can use some dynamite," Nicholas suggested once another attempt to open the doors failed.

"Are you crazy?" Bethany asked. "That might cause a cave-in and we could lose everything forever."

"I'm only kidding." He wiped a spot of dust from her nose. "We're going to get it open."

"I know." She walked off and got two bottles of water out of the cooler and handed him one.

"Thank you."

She uncapped the other one and gulped some down. "Ah, that hit the spot." She sat down on one of the folding chairs as Nicholas resumed his tests. Andre and George were down in the hole with some of the people George's archeological friend Hathor sent over to help. They were using sand-blasting tools to work on the doors, while Hathor was busy with the magnetometer trying to judge the depth of the tomb. Mark, fortunately for her, had decided not to join them today and chose to stay in his hotel room out of the heat.

It had been a long week. The police had finally grown tired of questioning her about Al-Shar. Mark had finally grown tired of questioning her about Al-Shar, and she had finally given up any hopes of ever seeing him again. She sighed. She supposed she was still depressed about learning about her father's death the way she had. With one quick phone call home, she had heard all the gory details from her brother, who assured her that everything had been taken care of. It still hurt her that she had missed the funeral, but she knew in her heart that her father was smiling down on her from heaven for what she had done. She just wished he was there with her to share in the glory.

Her thoughts went back to Al-Shar. *So we had sex. That doesn't mean that he owes you a commitment.* Too bad she didn't remember any of it. She looked up toward the sky. It was dark, like it was about to rain. That wasn't a good sign...not while they were excavating. "Nicholas," she called.

Nicholas looked up. "Yes?"

Bethany pointed to the sky. "It looks like rain."

He followed her fingers up to the sky and nodded. "Yes, it does."

"Maybe you ought to go down in the hole and let the others know."

"Okay." He put down his pad. "I'll be back in a minute." He climbed down the now secured ladder.

Thunder rumbled in the distance. She rose, not liking the sound of it. Rain could produce too many complications. If the water got down into the hole it could wash out or destroy everything down there. The skies rumbled again as the men climbed out of the hole. "It's about to pour," she told them. "What are we going to do?"

Hathor rushed over. "I've got tarp in the truck. We need to lay it and secure it before the rain comes down."

Some men from the working crew hurried over to the truck and hauled the tarp out.

"They know what to do," Hathor assured her. He radioed for Feneas and the police escort. "We're heading back to the bungalow. It's about to rain. We're loading all the equipment up now, so there's no need for you to make the trip back here."

"Okay," Feneas said through the radio. "I'll call you later."

∾

"I would kill for some waffles right now," Nicholas said as they climbed back into the cars the next morning. The rains were gone and the sun beamed down on them with a fury.

Bethany dug into her bag. "Would you settle for a granola bar?"

Nicholas brushed her hand away. "No, I would not. That stuff tastes like cardboard and it gives me the runs."

Bethany giggled. "You're crazy."

"Yeah, but you love me anyway."

Bethany opened the breakfast bar and bit a piece. Oh, well, she guessed absence did make the heart grow fonder. She thought she actually saw tears in his eyes when she stepped into the bungalow the night she returned with Mark. "I wonder how much damage was done to the site." She chewed and looked out of the window to avoid making a comment on what he just said. They knew the way to the excavation so well that they really didn't need the guides anymore, but they kept them anyway.

"Hopefully none," Feneas replied from the front seat. "You've come too far now to let a little rain stop you."

She smiled. That's why they kept him. He was so positive about everything, and he wasn't afraid to talk to her anymore. George had told her that he and his friends had searched the desert and the mountains for days for her after she disappeared.

Nicholas touched her hair. "When are you going to change the color back?"

"Maybe this weekend, if I can find the right shade."

"I'm pretty partial to redheads. With that rocking tan you have now, those pretty blue eyes, and red hair, you can make my fantasy come true."

"Mark wouldn't let you get that close to me," she reminded him.

Nicholas moved over in his seat. "You would have to bring up his name. Have you ever found out why he's here?"

"Nope. He keeps saying that he came just to find me, but you and I know better." She had cried on Nicholas' shoulder for days after Mark left her.

"So, he found you. Why is he still here? I'm sure he's claimed the reward by now."

"I was wondering the same thing. I told my brother to pay him off just to get rid of him. I hope Mark doesn't think I'm going back with him."

"I hope you don't."

"No. I've gotten him out of my system." *And replaced him.*

They arrived at the site before the rest of the excavation team. Bethany and the others climbed out and started checking the area for damage. George, Andre and Hathor removed the tarp and then Hathor climbed down the hole. He returned a few minutes later. "There's a little water, but it is okay. No major damage."

"Can I go down today?" Bethany asked as the men unloaded the equipment. "I haven't been down there since the rescue squad pulled me out."

"Okay," George agreed. "I think it is safe enough."

Bethany stood and stared at the golden doors that she could now see clearly because of the special lighting that had been installed. The royal seal was still intact. The others had been busy since her disappearance, carting off the dirt and debris and securing the place. She ran her hand along the etching on the plaque. "What does it say?" she asked Hathor.

"Beware. Do not disturb the sleep of Amasis."

"That sounds like a curse."

"Hathor laughed. "Yes, it is, but only to those who believe."

"And you don't."

"Nope. It was used as a way to keep looters out."

"So, do you think he's really in there? All the books I've read said he was from Sais."

"His tomb was never found there. I believe that this is it."

Bethany pulled at one of the doors. "What is it sealed with, some ancient glue?" There was a loud creak and then the door opened. "Oh, oh." Hot air escaped from the chamber.

"Whoopee!" Hathor shouted. "You did it." He ran to the ladder and hollered up. "George, Andre, Nicholas. Bethany has opened the doors." He turned to Bethany. "Don't go inside. We're going to do this together."

Bethany backed away from the doors and then froze in place. Something shiny and gold glittered at her from beyond the door. George and the others shimmed down the ladder. George hugged her. "You did it."

"But she's a girl," Nicholas pouted. "How did she do that?"

"The same way she discovered it," Andre told him. "Dumb luck."

"I'm scared," Bethany said. "I think my life is about to change."

Nicholas ruffled her hair. "For the best. We're going to be fricken famous."

"Pull up your respirators," Andre ordered. "They will help provide a flow of air and help you stay cool in this heat." He pulled the white full faced masked over his head and tied it around his throat. He adjusted the motorized battery pack at his waist so he could move around comfortably.

George and Andre did the same thing and then George pulled on the left door, while Andre pulled on the right. Both doors opened all the way. An overwhelming stale stench poured out. Bethany secured the respirator on her nose, walked up to the door and peeped in.

"What do you see?" George asked.

"Lots and lots of gold."

"Whoopee," Hathor exclaimed. "Let's go in."

"Don't you think we should radio the find in first to the Supreme Council of Antiquities?" Andre asked.

"Oh yeah. I forgot in all the excitement."

"Let's go," Hathor said once the crew had arrived from the council. He adjusted the light on his hard hat and led them into the tunnel.

It was dark and musty, Bethany noticed as they walked. But unlike Ramesses VI's tomb, this one had a lot of stairs. She couldn't imagine doing this on a day to day basis as the builders had. The artwork on the walls was exceptionally beautiful, beginning with the Book of the Dead. The place was a great cloistered building of stone and it was decorated with pillars carved with imitation palm trees and other costly objects. They stopped before another set of doors also held shut by a royal seal.

"I think this is it," Hathor announced. Word spread to the last person in line with them. Two men from the council came to the front of the line to examine the seal.

"It's official," he said. "From the 26th Dynasty."

Bethany and the others cheered. They cheered even more when the seal was broken and the doors opened. The royal burial sepulcher was just beyond the doors.

"Look at all this stuff," George said from behind his respirator. "He was fricken rich."

Bethany agreed as the crew went in began to examine the little golden statues, thrones, cabinets and stools. Bethany found a chest of jewelry. She picked up one of the pieces. It was a golden ring decorated with scarabs. In the center sat a huge sapphire. She gently placed it back inside the chest. George and Hathor went off to look at another chamber to the right. They returned a few minutes later announcing that they had found the sarcophagus. She followed the others into the chamber. The sarcophagus was there, but it was enshrined in stone, which meant some experts had to come in and remove it.

Andre patted her hand. "Don't look so disappointed. You'll get to see it as soon as the professionals come to dig it out. We don't want to ruin it by trying to do it ourselves."

"I'm not that disappointed," she said. She pointed. "Look... another chamber." She and Andre walked over and peeped inside. "It's the death mask and personal effects." Chests and chests of jewelry, statues, and figures of Anubis lined this chamber. There was another throne, golden ankhs and a canopic chest, which held the mummy's vital organs. "I can't wait until they finish digging this stuff out," she replied. "I wonder how many other chambers are in here."

"Too many to discover today," Andre replied. "I think our stay in Egypt is going to be a bit longer than we expected."

"Something came for you today," George told Bethany about a week after their historical find was announced. He handed her the registered letter.

"It looks important," she replied. She opened the envelope only to find another envelope with an official seal. "Ooh, I feel special." She broke the seal and pulled the letter out and read it aloud. "You are cordially invited to attend a formal reception in your honor." Bethany stopped reading and squealed. "We've been invited to King Amasis' palace for a benefit in our honor."

"We know," Andre said entering the room. "We got our invitations too."

"What am I going to wear? I don't have anything fancy with me."

"Not our problem," Nicholas said as he sat down at the breakfast table across from her. "All we have to do is rent a tux. Everything else we need is included in the package deal."

Bethany put down the envelope and bit into her wheat toast. "You guys are so lucky. I have to buy a gown and shoes, and get my hair done."

"The reception is this Saturday, and today is Thursday. You don't have very much time."

"Okay, which one of you guys is going to volunteer to go shopping with me?"

"Not me," the trio replied simultaneously.

"Why not? It will be fun. We'll do lunch." She still couldn't get any takers. "That's okay. I'll go by myself, and I'll take a leisurely stroll through the lingerie section and try on a couple of things. Of course I'll have to ask the salesgirl for her opinion on how they look on me."

Nicholas raised an eyebrow.

"Forget it," she replied. "You missed the opportunity."

CHAPTER 13

*W*hy didn't she have any female friends? It would be fun to go shopping with another woman who could offer sane advice on what to wear. Feneas had dropped her off at the most prestigious shopping district in Luxor and he told her to call him when she was finished. She had an appointment at the hairdresser tomorrow at two, which meant another trip back, but first she had to choose a fancy gown. Bethany walked in and out of stores, looking and occasionally trying on a couple of things. Then she stepped inside of a boutique where she was nearly run over by saleswomen who for some reason knew who she was and wanted to help her. She chose a young woman who was closer to her age and build, and promised to see some of the others for help with shoes and accessories.

"My name is Armana," the young woman said a few minutes later. "This is my boutique."

"Help me, Armana. I need something wonderful to wear to a formal party at the king's palace."

"I know," Armana said. "You're the talk of the town. You got kidnapped and was held hostage by some handsome bandit, and then you found that tomb. I'd be delighted to help you."

"I'm flattered, I think." She hadn't thought of Al-Shar in weeks since her return. "Now you see why I can't go there in cargo pants and a camp shirt. I don't have enough time to wait until I can get something made. I need something fast."

Armana went into the back and came out with a lovely off white gown and handed it to Bethany. "I think this might be perfect."

Bethany took the gown and dashed into the fitting room. The gown was beautiful and the fit was perfect, but she had a problem with the color. She was expecting her period any day now and didn't want any little shockers at the palace. She expected it two days ago, but she guessed it was late from all the excitement and the trauma of being kidnapped. Not to mention climbing in and out of holes and being in the desert heat for hours at a time. She removed the gown and handed it back to Armana.

"I think I need to try something in a darker color. It's that time of the month and I don't want any little surprises."

Armana agreed. "Perfectly understandable. Black would be perfect. It's formal, but you're much too young to wear such a blah color. Let me see what I can find." She dashed out and came back later with an armful of gowns. Hours later Bethany had made a decision. Her next stop was to find the perfect pair of shoes. At five feet seven she didn't really need anything too high, but they had to be comfortable enough to dance in. Many more hours later Feneas arrived to help her carry all her bags and boxes out of the stores and load them into the back on the SUV.

Nicholas was waiting outside of the bungalow when they drove up. "Did you leave anything on the shelves?"

"Yes, smarty pants."

He helped her unload the car. "It doesn't look like it."

"I needed a few things."

"Like lingerie? Are you planning on bagging yourself a prince?"

"Not likely," she replied. "Unless there's one in that sarcophagus we unearthed."

"Speaking of which, the museum called while you were out. They've opened it. It wasn't a prince."

"Don't tell me that it's empty." She flopped down in a chair when the last bag made it inside.

"Nope. They think it is a king. They're ninety-eight percent sure that it is, but they won't know for sure until they do a couple more tests."

"Whew, it's still something to celebrate."

~

"What are the chances that Ms. Dailet would find something your people have been searching for centuries for?" Jamaal asked Yahi as they practiced archery in an open field behind the palace.

"About a billion to one. She has more luck than sense."

"Now is that any way to talk about the guest of honor at tonight's party."

"Is that tonight?" He aimed at the target, pulled the bow string and let the arrow sail through the air. It hit the bull's eye dead center. "I suppose that I will have to attend."

"Yes, you do. It is part of your duty as a prince."

"Well if I must I must."

Jamaal aimed at the target and shot. The arrow landed just beneath Yahi's. "I wonder if she'll be bringing a date."

"I have a weapon in my hand," Yahi threatened him.

Jamaal smiled. "But what if she does?"

"Then I will act accordingly."

"Which means you are going to sulk?"

"Exactly." He rearmed his bow and let the arrow go. This one was a little off. It hit the side of the bull's eye.

"You're distracted all of a sudden. Is it because she might arrive with her fiancé?"

"Bethany is free to bring whomever she chooses."

"What about you? Are you bringing a date?"

Yahi shook his head. "No, I am a prince. That means the women will be there."

"Will I offend you if I gag myself with this arrow?"

Yahi smiled. "No, go right ahead."

"Yahi!"

Both men looked behind them. Princess Kasia came strolling across the green in a striking tennis outfit and a pair of sneakers. Her long brown hair was pulled back in a tail, and the rest was hidden behind a tennis visor.

"Yes, baby sis."

"Father is looking for you."

"So, you came all the way out here just to find me."

"Yes, I'm very considerate that way," she yelled.

"The two of you are definitely siblings," Jamaal whispered before Kasia reached them. "You're looking well princess Kasia."

"Thanks, Jamaal. I do try." She spun around. "Do you like my new tennis outfit? It's the latest rage at Wimbledon."

"It looks positively smashing on you," Jamaal answered using a British accent. "All eyes will be on you today at your match."

Yahi rolled his eyes at the sky. *Have mercy, the poor fool is so besotted with the infant.*

"What do you think, Yahi?" his sister asked.

"It makes your ass look big. Does it come in black? That would be more slimming."

Kasia rolled her eyes at him. "You're just jealous because my legs are better than yours. Tell him, Jamaal."

"I cannot lie, Yahi. Kasia's legs are phenomenal. Yours are cute, but they don't compare to hers."

Kasia batted her eyes at Jamaal. "Why thank you. I never realized that you even noticed me."

Yahi yawned. The two of them had been in love since they were kids, but they both were too stupid to acknowledge it.

"Can I tell Father that you are on your way?"

"Yes. I'll be there as soon as we put away the equipment."

Kasia turned to leave but then looked at Jamaal. "See you later at the party."

"Goodbye, Princess."

Kasia left them, swinging her hips more than usual.

Jamaal just sighed and began retrieving the bows and arrows and putting them up.

"Either you tell her how you feel or I will," Yahi threatened.

"You wouldn't dare."

"I don't understand what the problem is. You've known her since the day she was born. What's stopping you from asking her out?"

"She's a princess and I'm the son of a servant woman."

"Fathered by Emir Hatem."

"This means that I'm a bastard."

"You're that without parentage," Yahi teased.

Jamaal smiled weakly.

"Kasia doesn't care about that and you know it. Emir wanted to legitimize you years ago, but you have refused."

"I do not want to get into Khalaf's way to the throne. As for Kasia, Khalaf wants her too."

"No, he doesn't. You know Khalaf. He wants every woman who crosses his path. But the fact is Khalaf likes being single. Go on, ask her out and stop torturing yourself."

"We better get back. Your father is expecting you."

The throne room was empty for a change, except for his father. "Come on up here boy, and sit down next to me. I think we need to talk."

Yahi went up the stairs and sat down on the queen's throne. "About what?"

"Your future."

"We both know what that is already. I'll be king the moment you take your last breath."

Waheed laughed. "Have I said it that many times?"

Yahi nodded. It was best not to say much and just listen. "Well, at the rate you're going you might go before me."

"What do you mean by that?" The king sighed. "You know, there's not many things that go on in this country I don't know about. And it's not every day I find out that my son has been less than honest with me."

"I have never lied to you, Father."

"No, you just leave out things that you don't want me to know about."

Yahi smiled innocently. "Like what?"

"Like your little adventures at the cemeteries, and brawling with criminals."

Yahi opened his mouth to explain but the king cut him off.

"I know you think what you're doing is right, and maybe it is, but you are a prince and you're going about it the wrong way." He looked over at his son. "At least you had the common sense to wear a disguise."

"How did you find out?"

"Not the way you think. No one ratted you out. I just put two and two together when the incidents were brought to my attention. I thought who would have enough access and connections to feed all those people? And who would be smart enough to do it and not get caught? Who can ride a horse like the dickens and escape the law every time? Yahi, you're a genius, but your plan backfired. They think you're a criminal."

Yahi lowered his head in shame. "I've never stolen or harmed anyone. In fact, Jamaal and I have been trying to stop the looting of the tombs. That's how it all got started. We wanted to protect the tombs of our kings and queens and the next thing we knew we were involved in several other things that we could do only in disguise. We haven't broken any laws."

"You're wanted for kidnapping and dealing in slave trade. Your mother would simply die if she found that out."

"I did not kidnap that woman. Jamaal found out about these two men who wanted to trade something valuable for horses. Of course we thought it would be something stolen, like some artifacts from the tombs, but then it turned out to be a woman. I didn't know what to do, but I knew I had to get her away from them before she was harmed."

"How many horses did you trade?"

"Ten."

"She must be something special if you traded ten horses for her."

Yahi agreed. "I said the same thing to Jamaal. That was a lot of horseflesh to trade for a woman."

The king laughed. "So, what happened next?"

"Things got really blown out of proportion because I recognized her the moment I saw her face. A couple of days earlier I nearly ran over her with a horse while trying to escape some police."

The king groaned.

"It really wasn't as bad as it sounds, but Jamaal and I were in this cemetery delivering food and the police saw us leaving and thought we were robbing the graves so they chased us through the bazaar in Cairo. That's when I nearly ran over this woman. I stopped to make sure she was okay and then we rode off."

"Continue."

"Well she recognized me too after Maaches and Sabola left. That's the name of the men who traded her. They had drugged her up with something, which apparently wore off and then she lit into me, calling me all kinds of names, and accusing me of being a bandit and a kidnapper. I was pissed because I couldn't believe that this was the same woman I had run into earlier. I don't believe in coincidences, so I thought she was a spy for the police who were trying to catch me."

"So what happened after that?"

"Well, I kind of threw her in the harem."

"You did what?"

"I put her in the harem under Keis and Jabari."

"What were you thinking Yahi?"

"That I'd let her cool off. I had all the intentions in the world of returning her to her hotel where they kidnapped her from when I found out who she was. Then the next day I learned that she was an archeologist for the United States and that her family was looking for her. I tried calling her father, and then I learned that someone had murdered him the day before."

"Murdered him?"

Yahi nodded. "Yes. I thought that whoever killed her father might have something to do with the kidnapping. So that is why I couldn't return her."

"Were you afraid that the police might think that you were involved with her father's murder?"

"No, I thought whomever killed him might come after her."

Waheed thought about what he had just heard. He rubbed his bearded chin and watched Yahi fidget around on the other throne like he used to do as a kid when they had these types of conversations. The boy had been a handful even back then. But he had a kind and generous heart and wouldn't harm a fly.

"I didn't mean for it to get so out of control, but as far as I know only a few people know the truth, and they are loyal."

"That may be so, but there's always a chance that one of them might accidentally slip up. Now tell me, how did you get her from the harem to where we are today?"

"I finally made up my mind to take her back, but I had to go see Emir first because I promised him that I'd come for a visit. So I took her with me."

The king frowned. "You took a kidnap victim to see Emir? What did he have to say about that?"

"Emir adores her."

"My best friend would."

"Well, she got to meet everyone and she kept trying to find out what I look like. Khalaf met her and she danced for us."

"The hostage danced for you? What kind of dance?"

"A belly dance. You should have seen it. She was wonderful."

"Continue."

"There was a lot of smoking and eating and…"

"Yes, skip all that. I know what kinds of parties my friend throws. I'm sure there was a lot of food and music."

"Yes, and I got really high and didn't remember what happened and the next thing I knew it was morning and the woman and I left. Then we got ambushed by two men on our way back to Luxor. We were in the mountains and they started shooting at us. Of course, Bethany and I argued about who they were after, since she reasoned that I had made my fair share of enemies. But I told her that I thought that they were after her because she had reward money for her safe return. We were arguing when a third man appeared from out of nowhere with a gun."

Waheed laughed. "I don't think he could have snuck upon the two of you if you weren't arguing. Continue."

"Well the other two men caught up and it turned out to be Sabola and Maaches."

"The men who traded Bethany to you and who originally kidnapped her?"

Yahi nodded. "Can you believe that they tried to pin it on me? Well the man turned out to be Bethany's fiancé from America."

Waheed continued to laugh. "This is getting better by the moment. What else?"

"Well, he took our guns away and was going to tie me up, but then I got away."

Waheed stopped laughing. "How did you manage to do that?"

"With a little help from my friends. Basil called me earlier at Emir to let me know about what was going to happen. He overheard it when the Maaches and Sabola passed through his caravan on the way to find me."

"So you knew about them looking for you before you left Emir's palace?"

Yahi nodded. "I had to leave Emir before the fools tried to come there and try something. I had enough people involved and I didn't want to involve them too. So I told Basil to round up some help and to meet me in the mountains."

"So that is when you let the young woman go?"

Yahi nodded. "I knew her fiancé would get her back safely."

"What happened to Sabola and Maaches?"

"Basil took them to the police and they confessed."

"Whew. Well, at least you're not guilty of kidnapping anymore."

"No, but I did hold her against here will for a couple of nights."

"You let me take care of that." He paused. "Why didn't you come to me in the beginning?"

"I was afraid that you wouldn't understand. You are so busy being king that I thought I could help out a few people without involving you."

"I am never too busy for you. Do you understand that? I had no idea that we have people living in cemeteries. I'll take care of that too. I'll find them homes and food."

"Thanks, father. So what am I supposed to do now?"

"Al-Shar Khan has to go into hiding for a while until all of this blows over."

Yahi nodded. "I understand. The beard itches anyway."

"You're incorrigible and you've dragged poor Jamaal in this with you too."

Yahi shrugged his shoulders. "Speaking of Jamaal, what do you think about him?"

"I have loved him like a son since the day he was born. Why?"

"He's in love with Kasia."

"Boy, everyone in the kingdom knows that except for Kasia. He's been following her around like a little puppy since the day she took her first step."

"So you would have no problem with them dating."

"No, in fact I'd welcome it. He loves her and would make her a splendid husband. Why?"

"I feel the same way, but Jamaal thinks that he is below Kasia because his mother was our servant."

"That's silly. He's my best friend's child...second in line for a throne. Even Nailah loves him, and there aren't too many women who would accept another woman's child as her own."

"I agree with you, but Jamaal doesn't see it that way."

"You think I need to talk to him."

Yahi nodded. Jamaal hadn't had any quality time with his father in some time, which always made Jamaal nervous. Yahi smiled. Why should he be the only one to suffer? "Yes, I think you need to have a good long heart to heart talk with him."

"I will talk to him now and give him my blessing. Find him and send him in. After that the rest is up to him. He's the one who actually has to ask Kasia out."

Yahi rose. "The poor fool. She is going to drive him crazy."

Waheed laughed. "Yes, she most certainly will."

CHAPTER 14

"*I*sn't she ready yet?" Nicholas asked Andre when he joined them in the foyer.

Andre shook his head. "You know women. They have many other things to do to get ready then we men do."

Feneas had arrived and was waiting with George and Hathor on the other side of the room. He had rented a limousine to take them to the reception, which he too would be attending because he was a part of the historical find.

"Maybe I should go up and get her," Nicholas suggested.

"No need," Bethany said as she appeared. "I hope I didn't keep you guys waiting too long.

The men rose. Nicholas gulped. "You look like a princess."

Bethany giggled. "I feel like one." They got back in the car and headed back to Cairo.

Bethany stared in wide-eyed wonder as the limousine drove through the gates of the royal compound. Even at night, it was a glorious sight to see. Armed guards dressed in white and khaki light-weight uniforms manned the gates and towers. The area was lined with trees and shrubbery that could withstand the torturous heat. Feneas drove the limousine up a paved roadway that led them through acres and acres of well-manicured landscape.

There were several outer buildings, a tennis court, and some stables. A guard appeared in the middle of the road. Feneas stopped, flashed his visitor's pass, and then was allowed to continue. "We're almost there, I think," he announced. He continued along the road, which began to veer to the right.

Bethany looked straight ahead, wanting to get a good view from a distance of the palace. "Look at the size of this place," she shouted enthusiastically as the palace appeared in front of them. It was a big white building with steeples, domes, archways, and marbled columns. Huge carved statues of Egyptian pharaohs decorated the top of the stairs. Like the gates, the palace was heavily guarded. These were dressed more formally in black uniforms bearing the royal family official crest. One of them stepped forward as soon as Feneas stopped and showed his pass. He called for a valet who arrived to take the limousine, while another young man appeared to get their luggage. There were hundreds of other cars arriving, and the news media had beaten them there. They took pictures of the group as they stepped from the limousine and continued to photograph or film their every move. Bethany picked up the hem of her gown and followed the people who had come to greet them as they made their way through the palace door. *I bet Prince Charming's palace has nothing on this place.* She entered, ogling the large reception area.

"Right this way, Ms. Dailet," a young woman about twenty years old said to her. "My name is Kelpri, and I am to act as your guide and liaison to the royal family during your stay. Is everyone here?"

"Yes," Bethany answered. "We're all here."

"Okay, then follow me."

Bethany and the others followed Kelpri down a long corridor. She stopped abruptly by a door. "This is the throne room. Don't be nervous, but I think I need to inform all of you that there are a lot of people inside waiting to meet you. When you meet the royal family, it is proper protocol for the men to bow and for the women to curtsy."

Bethany's stomach pitched with butterflies.

"You are to address them as Your Highness and you are only supposed to entertain them with conversation when you are spoken to."

"I hope I can remember all that," Nicholas whispered to her.

Kelpri opened the door and someone announced their arrival.

Bethany squeezed Nicholas' hand. "Okay, here we go."

Camera flashes went off in their faces, temporarily blinding them. There was a variety of guests from across Africa and a few who appeared to be Americans. Bethany and the other archeologists were mobbed as they made it to the reception line. Autograph books and newspaper articles were pushed at them for their signature, which delighted all of them, except Feneas who seemed a bit nervous. "Just relax and enjoy it," Bethany whispered to her friends. Out of the corner of her eye she could see the royal thrones, but they appeared empty. Finally, after answering tons of questions they made their way to the front of the reception line.

"Welcome, Ms. Dailet," a man said to her. "I am Waheed Amasis and I have been waiting to meet you for some time now."

Bethany curtsied. "Your Highness."

"Rise, dear," Waheed replied. He was very tall, and dressed in a black tuxedo. "Who are these wonderful people with you?"

Bethany made the introductions. The king shook all of their hands and welcomed them to the palace. "Now I would like you to meet my family if I can wrestle them away from the media. One by one, he introduced them. "This is my lovely wife, Naadirah, and my daughter Kasia, and my godson Jamaal." He joked. "I would introduce you to my son, but he has yet to put in an appearance."

Jamaal stepped forward. "He should be arriving shortly. He is on the phone with my father."

He's cute, Bethany noticed as she studied him. Tall, short dark hair, soulful brown eyes and a dark tan. Now why does he look so familiar?

"The reception is going to move to the dining room," Waheed announced. "Hopefully my son will join us there."

The room was big enough to seat over one hundred and fifty people. The royals spread out at different tables to make polite conversation with the rest of the guests. Bethany and her group were lucky enough to share a table with the king. He sat her to his right while the chair to his left remained empty. Moments later the door opened and someone entered and was announced.

"Prince Yahi Amasis."

To turn around would have been rude, so Bethany just sat forward and waited, hoping that the empty seat was for him.

"I was beginning to think that you would miss dinner," Waheed said when the young man arrived.

"I had to take a very important phone call."

"Never mind, we'll discuss it later. I want you to meet someone. Yahi, this is Ms. Bethany Dailet,"

Bethany raised her eyes and stared into the face of a man who was so handsome her heart skipped a beat or two. *Breathe*, she ordered in her head. She rose to get the circulation going again and curtsied. "Your Highness."

He bowed to her. "Please call me Yahi."

Bethany smiled and he smiled back at her revealing perfect straight teeth. He was dressed in a black tux with gold brocade trim, tailored to fit his magnificent body. He was tall like his father.

"Please be seated," the king whispered. "People are starting to stare. The two of you will have later to get acquainted."

Bethany could hardly eat as she studied him from beneath lowered lashes.

He was blond haired and blue eyed like his mother, with a clean-shaven face. His look was classically Egyptian with a straight nose and a strong chin. Every now and then she caught him looking at her when he thought she wasn't looking at him. She couldn't remember what the hell she ate, but she would never forget that face.

After dinner Kelpri showed them to the rooms where they would be staying. They were allowed a couple of minutes to relax and freshen up and they would be taken to the ballroom for dancing. The room assigned to her had mahogany furniture that was polished to a high gleam. The bed and windows bore matching fabrics, a deep burgundy with gold thread. Bethany walked over to the bathroom door and opened it. Inside she found the usual things, a toilet, and a sink. A sunken tub with gold fixtures. Her eyes widened. It was the type of tub she dreamed about. She used the restroom, fixed her hair and makeup and then went back into the room to wait. Someone knocked before she got comfortable.

"Come in."

The door opened and Prince Yahi walked in.

Bethany rose. "Your highness."

"I thought I told you to call me Yahi."

"Yes, Yahi."

"Do you like your room?"

"Yes, it's lovely. Especially the tub."

He nodded. "I'm kind of partial to taking nice long soaks myself," he confessed. "I have come to escort you to the ballroom." He presented his arm to her and she accepted it. "What about the others?" she asked as they left the room.

"They have already been taken there." They walked down a series of halls. Each wall was lined with oil paintings and family portraits.

"Do you like being a prince?" she asked.

"Sometimes I despise it," he replied. "Tonight is not one of those nights." He chuckled.

This is odd, she thought. That chuckle sounded familiar. She brushed it off. His voice was deep, refined, and cultured she noted as they talked. They discussed her find as they walked.

"The media claims you fell down a hole and just happened to discover the hidden tomb. Is that correct?"

"Yes, that's exactly how it happened. I was checking out some dirt samples and talking with one of the other archeologist when I noticed how soft the ground was under my feet. The next thing I knew the ground seemed to open up and suck me right in. I thought it was quick sand, and then I landed on my feet right in front of these two big golden doors."

"It sounds like something out of an adventure movie," he replied. "But I'm glad you didn't get hurt."

She chuckled. "Just my pride. I have always been a bit of a klutz."

They stopped outside the ballroom where the music sounded festive. There was laughter and shouting and everyone sounded like they were having a good time. "Shall we enter?"

Bethany nodded. She slid her arm from his. Prince Yahi opened both doors and then stepped aside to get her reaction. "Wow, I feel like Cinderella."

"Do you waltz, Cinderella?"

"Yes, Prince Charming, I do."

Yahi pulled her as close to him as humanly possible while doing the waltz. He had considered her beautiful from the first time he laid eyes on her, but all dressed up he could not find the proper word. Oh yes, elegant, and she smelled like flowers. She had gotten rid of the black dye job that Eboni had given her and gone back to her natural hair color, but not exactly. It was a darker shade of blonde, with red highlights that gave her a more exotic look, and made her baby blue eyes the center of attention.

He waltzed her around, taking precautions not to run into the other couples dancing nearby. Like the belly-dance she had performed for him over a month ago, her waltz was perfect and so was her tango he discovered later. Finally, the band played a slow number. Yahi pulled her to him until their bodies melded. His body reacted on contact. Maybe it was the way she looked in the royal blue gown that showed off her bust and small waist that had his blood boiling, or maybe it was the scent of her skin, or maybe his body had a better memory of what happened between them than his mind had. Whatever it was had him hooked.

"So where is this fiancé of yours?' he asked trying to get some control over his penis which was trying to rise at the most inopportune moment. The music ended and he started walking her back to where her friends were.

"The media tends to over-exaggerate," Bethany replied. "Mark and I used to be engaged, but he dumped me for a woman with more money. As for his whereabouts, hopefully he's on his way back to the United States to spend some of the reward money he collected for my safe return."

Yahi smiled. She still had that fiery temper. That is what drew him to her the most. That and that killer rack. "What kind of idiot would dump a beautiful woman like you?"

"Thanks for the compliment and the dance."

Yahi helped her into her seat, bowed, and then walked away.

"The prince appears smitten with our little Bethany," George replied once they were alone.

"He is not," Bethany said in her defense. "How can he be? We've just met."

Andre agreed with George. "It is the Bethany curse. The one she uses on the students back at the university. One look into those big blue eyes and men fall at her feet." He chuckled. "He had this big smile of his face the whole time the two of you were dancing."

Bethany fanned herself. "I don't know why? We were talking about me falling down the hole and Mark."

"Both very funny situations," Andre replied. "But he still has the hots for you."

Nicholas grumbled beside her. "I don't find either situation funny, and who does the prince think he is hogging our Bethany from us?"

George raised an eyebrow. "From us or from you?"

"Whatever. Granted the two of them did look good on the dance floor, but he has to learn to share."

Bethany leaned over and sniffed. "Are you drunk?"

"Probably."

"Where did you get liquor? Egypt is almost a dry country."

Nicholas opened his jacket lapel and exposed several small bottles of rum.

"You are going to get us arrested. I think smuggling liquor into the country is illegal."

"So what are they going to do to me, throw me in jail?"

"Yes, they might."

He rose. "Not if I go sleep it off first. I'm going to my room. It's been a long day." He bid everyone goodnight and left.

"Poor fellow," Andre replied. "He has loved and lost."

Bethany pouted. "You are not going to make me feel bad for this. I haven't led him on or anything."

George shook his head. "You haven't discouraged him either. You need to tell him you have no interest in him in that way so he can go on with his life."

"Don't the two of you think I know this? I don't want to hurt his feelings. Nicholas is like my best friend, and he's been there for me, but I'm not in love with him. In fact, he's like a brother to me."

"Don't tell him that," Hathor warned. "Men don't like that. It's almost as bad as it's not you, it's me."

"So it's all back in my lap now? I'll tell him once we get back to Luxor."

"I would say maybe you could fix him up with the princess, but looks like she's taken." George pointed toward the dance floor. Princess Kasia had her head against Jamaal's chest, and both of their eyes were closed. They were obviously enjoying each other's company and the dance. The royal family also watched, apparently delighted by what they saw. Prince Yahi waved to her which drew a little more attention from the media than she liked.

"I told you that he's infatuated with you," George said matter-of-factly.

"Nonsense," Bethany said as she waved back. "He's just being friendly."

Andre laughed. "Ooh little Bethany. Look at how he's smiling. Prince Yahi is planning to rock your world."

"Would you like a tour of the palace?" Yahi asked her later that evening. Most of the older folks had either gone home or gone up to bed. She had considered doing the same thing before he approached.

"I don't know. It's getting late."

"Aw, come on. It's not that late."

How could she refuse those dimples? "Okay."

He helped her out of her seat. "Would you care to see the outside of the palace or the inside of the palace?"

"What is the difference, besides the obvious reasons?"

"One may be quite boring, while the other might be quite interesting."

"I'm for the interesting one."

"That would be the outside tour. It is an excellent choice." He led her to the front reception room. Kelpri was still on duty, and obviously infatuated with the prince.

"What can I do for you, sir?"

"Please have the carriage sent to the front door. Ms. Dailet would like a tour of the grounds."

"Yes, sir. I can be ready to show her around in ten minutes." She rewarded him with a brilliant smile.

"That's okay," he replied, smiling back at her. "I will conduct the tour myself."

Kelpri looked at Bethany like she had personally put a knife in her back and turned it. "But sir, it is my job, and besides you're the prince."

"Yes, I know all that, but Ms. Dailet and I have much to discuss about her exciting find. It's business, you know."

Kelpri looked as though she was about to argue with him but then thought about it. "Yes, sir. I will send for the carriage."

"Thank you."

The carriage and coachman were waiting for them when they exited the palace. It was one of those topless types, with the royal crest and coat of arms on the polished brown doors. It was drawn by two white horses with plumes on their heads. "Your carriage awaits, Cinderella." Yahi escorted her down the stairs and helped her inside. He took the reins from the coachman and climbed up beside her. "I shall return it in excellent condition."

"No wheelies," the coachman replied.

"No, none indeed. I will be most gentle with the twins."

Bethany looked at him oddly.

"An old and very funny story, involving me and my rowdiness."

The coachman winked at him. "Be careful with this one."

Bethany blushed.

The coachman waved good-bye and then headed up the stairs to the palace. The prince shook the reins and the horses pranced. "This palace was designed by Belgian architect Ernest Jaspar," he began as they continued along the front. "In nineteen-ten it was transformed into an elite hotel where royalty and famous people stayed while visiting Cairo. It featured four-hundred rooms. In nineteen-eighty the hotel got converted back into a palace, and then my family moved in."

Bethany listened carefully. His voice was soothing and a bit whimsical. She could listen to him speak forever.

"Over there," he said pointing to the left "is one of the two tennis courts." He trotted the horses over in its direction. "It is where my sister humiliates me every chance she gets."

"Is she that good?"

He nodded. "She's a pro. She has been competing since she was ten." He paused. "Do you play?"

"Me? No, I never had the time to learn."

"That's a shame. It's very good exercise." They continued on. "Over there is one of the swimming pools. Did you bring your suit?"

"No, I wasn't instructed to do so."

"I can remedy that. It's one of my jobs to make sure that the pool house is stocked with suits. I am sure I can find one that will fit."

"You did not ask me if I can swim."

"Can you?"

"Like a fish," she replied.

"Good, then we will take a dip before the night is over."

She smiled. He was so silly. "What's that?" she asked as they came upon a small building."

"A museum."

"You have your own museum."

"Just a small one. My father likes to collect things. Would you like to see it?"

"Yes."

He drove the carriage over to it, climbed out, tied up the horses and then helped her down. He led her inside and he turned on the lights.

"It's Egyptian artifacts."

"Yes, from the 26th Dynasty. It belongs to an ancient ancestor of ours."

"I know. I think I've met him recently."

Yahi grabbed her arm. "What do you mean? Have you opened the tomb?"

Bethany nodded. "I think we found your ancestor."

Yahi's smile brightened. "My father will be pleased, but how can you be sure?"

She walked around and pointed to a chest. "I saw one exactly like this one inside the tomb."

"You've been inside."

"Yes. It's very big and has several chambers." She walked back over to him and took his hand. "I've also held the original copy of this." On his finger rested a gold scarab ring with a sapphire in the center.

"It is our family ring. Every male gets one when he reaches puberty. It is a tradition handed down since the reign of Pharaoh Amasis. I will give one to my son one day."

"Do you like children?"

"I'm crazy about them. I plan to have a kingdom full."

She looked into his eyes. "You're very optimistic."

"And hopefully potent," he teased.

Bethany stooped down. "What is this?"

"A golden cradle for a golden child. It was mine."

She rose. "Seems to reason that your stuff goes in here too. In one million years people will find it and go gaga over it."

Yahi laughed and her knees went weak. *Oh oh, this has only happened once before.* She hadn't thought about Al-Shar all evening. Maybe that was a good thing. He certainly wasn't worried about her.

"I would really like to see the tomb," Yahi announced as they left the museum.

"I will see to it that you do," Bethany replied. They rode to the back of the palace.

"This is where Kasia, Jamaal and I used to play as kids." It was a big playhouse with swings and a slide.

"Is Jamaal a relative?"

"Not by blood. Our fathers are best friends and we grew up together. He came to live with us after his mother died."

"That would explain why he was holding your sister so tenderly while they danced."

"You noticed?"

"I couldn't help it. They looked so good together. Have they been dating long?"

"Since today."

"What?"

"Yes, both of them have been in love forever, but Jamaal was a big chicken and too afraid to tell her how he felt until I made my father have a talk with him."

"You told on him?"

"I sure did. It was right after my father got through giving me one of those long boring speeches about being responsible and about what was going to happen one day when I become king. Then I told him about Jamaal." He laughed. "Why should I be the only one getting preached to?"

Bethany laughed. "He's going to get you for that."

"Yes, I know, but I couldn't help it. Jamaal was totally miserable to be around when he was mooning over Kasia."

"Are you and Jamaal close?"

"We're as thick as thieves."

CHAPTER 15

"Come out and let me see how the suit fits?" Yahi called to Bethany later.

"I don't think so. There's not much to it."

"I promise not to be judgmental."

"But you're a prince, and I don't know if it's proper." She came out of the pool house.

Yahi stared. No, it was positively indecent, and he loved it. "Oh, my, you are beautiful." Luckily, he was in the pool and she could not see his real reaction to the suit.

"I'm almost nude."

"You look like an Egyptian queen. Cleopatra would be envious." The bikini was black with a top that barely covered her generous breasts. The bottom was held together by tiny strings that rode her hips. Bethany stepped into the pool and he swam over to meet her. "Show me what you can do."

Bethany treaded water on her back away from him, tumbled and then came up on her stomach. She swam over to the other side of the pool and then back to him.

"You are a good swimmer."

"My father insisted that I take lessons. He didn't want me to spend all my time with my head buried in books."

Yahi swam over to the other end of the pool and then came back over to her.

"You're good too."

"Jamaal and I used to practice in the Nile. You would get real good too trying to keep away from crocodiles."

Bethany gasped. "Surely you jest?"

"No, it's all true. We used to do a lot of foolish things when we were young."

"It's hard to believe that a prince of Egypt could be so free. It's not how I envisioned that royalty behave."

He laughed. "My parents didn't expect it either. Especially when the police brought us home that day. Try to keep that out of the newspaper. The media had a field day."

"Horrid boy."

Yahi pulled her to him and kissed her. Bethany melted in his arms and then broke the kiss. "Is something wrong?"

"Not exactly."

"Is there someone else? You said you were no longer engaged."

"Yes, well, not exactly."

"Which is it?"

"There was someone."

"But there isn't anymore?"

"I don't know. I mean, I guess not. I haven't seen him in weeks."

He kissed her on the forehead. "What happened?"

"He sent me back to my life."

"I don't understand."

"Never mind."

He pulled her into his arms to comfort her. "I don't know if I can make you forget him, but I would like the chance to try."

"But you barely know me. We've only just met."

"That does not mean we can't be attracted to each other." He lowered his lips to hers. Bethany melted in his arms again. He did not mean for it to go this far but it was too late to stop kissing her. Her body was soft and it made his grow hard with need. He did not remember their last time together…just a rumpled bed and unsaid words the next morning, and then he gave her over to Mark Kauffman. He did not plan to ever do that again.

"Get a room, please," a very annoying voice said to them.

Bethany broke the kiss and hid behind him.

"Sister dear, you have the most aggravating sense of timing."

Kasia had arrived with Jamaal. She laughed. "Oh, are we interrupting something?

"Yes,"

"No," Bethany answered.

Jamaal chuckled. "I think we are."

Yahi changed his answer. "No, we were just swimming."

"With your lips?" Kasia asked sarcastically.

"Yes, I was practicing mouth-to-mouth necessitation."

Bethany punched him playfully on the arm. "That was horrible. I could have come up with something better than that, and I'm not very good at lying."

"What do the two of you want?"

"Kelpri is hysterical because you haven't returned. She said you took Ms. Dailet on the tour of the grounds and have been gone quite a while."

"Kelpri will get over it. We took the tour and decided to take a swim. Is there something wrong with that?"

"That depends. Are you naked?"

"No, I haven't been skinny dipping in years."

Bethany giggled. "This is humiliating."

Kasia smirked. "Why? My brother wants you badly. His eyes never left you from the time the two of you were introduced."

"That's enough, brat. Ms. Dailet does not want to hear about your take on my raging desire for her."

Bethany smirked. "Raging?"

"Oh yeah."

"Are you two coming out?" Jamaal asked.

"I don't think so," Bethany replied.

Jamaal bent forward and looked down in the water. "Are you naked?"

"Damn near," Yahi answered for her. "You should see the suit she's wearing. It will rock your world."

"Can I see it?" Kasia asked.

"My sister has this thing for clothes. Her future husband will go broke with the way she shops."

"It's indecent," Bethany told her.

"Yahi has seen you in it already and I'm a girl. I have the same thing you do."

"Yes, but no one else does," she said pointing at Jamaal."

Jamaal cleared his throat as he straightened up. "I promise I won't say anything."

"Okay." Bethany climbed out of the pool to model the suit for Kasia.

"Damn," Jamaal uttered.

"Thanks," Yahi replied. "That's the same thing I thought when I saw her in it. I purchased it with the rest of the suits for the guests, but I had no idea what it was going to look like."

Kasia walked around Bethany. "Maybe I ought to take you shopping with me the next time I go instead of mother. She would never allow me to buy anything so fetching."

"It's not just the suit," Jamaal stated. "The archeologist is built like a goddess."

"I thought you weren't going to say anything," Bethany told him. She tried to cover her assets.

Yahi laughed. "Too late. Jamaal has given his approval."

"Do you really like it, Jamaal?" Kasia asked.

"Yes, it is most becoming."

"Then I just have to have one like it. Does it come in red, Yahi?"

"Oh my," Jamaal replied.

"Yes, candy apple red."

"Where did you find it?"

"At a little boutique in France on my last visit there. I liked the label. It is by a designer named Dailet." He looked up at Bethany. "Any relation?"

"She was my mother. She died a couple of years ago."

"Your mother was a designer?" Kasia squealed. "You just have to tell me all about her."

The two women hurried back to the pool house for Bethany to change. Yahi climbed out of the pool, and Jamaal gave him that look "What were you thinking of doing to Ms. Dailet if we hadn't arrived?"

Yahi grabbed a towel and dried off. "A lot of depraved acts of a sexual nature."

"So you were about to move in on Al-Shar's woman. There is something kind of sick about that."

"I cannot help how I feel."

"That's just lust talking."

"I know, but it's more than that. I can't get her out of my thoughts."

"Did you see that bikini? I don't know about you, but I'm all tingly inside. I'll never forget how she looked when she stepped out of that pool."

"You just have to order one for Kasia....in red."

"Yuck. You're talking about my baby sister."

"Have you taken a look at her? She's rocking some serious curves. She's not a baby anymore."

"Gross, no, I don't look at her that way. That would be immoral."

Jamaal laughed. "Come on we have to get back to the palace before they come looking for us."

Mark read the headlines of the newspaper. "An Egyptian prince dances with an American goddess. American archeologist has not only won the admiration of the Egyptian people, but from the looks of things it appears that she has also caught the eye of Egypt's crowned prince, Yahi A. Amasis, heir to the Egyptian throne. Ms. Bethany Dailet and a team of archeologists recently discovered the tomb of what appears to be a king from the 26th Dynasty. It is rumored that it could be the ancestor of the prince, Pharaoh Amasis, whom the family has been searching for years. Ms. Dailet met the prince at a reception a couple of days ago given in her honor and it is rumored that the two of them were inseparable." Mark slammed the newspaper down on the table.

"Lies, all lies. Bethany would never go for a man like that." He picked the newspaper back up and continued to read aloud. "Ms. Dailet was kidnapped and held hostage for nearly two weeks until she was rescued by her fiancé, Mark Kauffman, and returned to her co-workers. Ms. Dailet's, father Ernest Dailet, also an archeologist was found dead at his home in Indianapolis, Indiana a couple of days after Bethany disappeared. Police suspect foul play, but no one has been taken into custody as of this printing. Ms. Dailet has been invited to attend a formal costume party given by a hotel in Luxor to commemorate the historical find on Saturday. All eyes will be on the media to find out if the prince will attend."

"A costume party? I wonder if I can swing an invitation. After all, I did rescue Bethany." Mark looked up the phone number to the hotel and dialed. He asked to speak to whoever was in charge of the party, explained who he was, and asked to be invited. The publicist for the hotel was only too happy to oblige. The tickets were to be delivered in a couple of days. Mark hung up the phone, smiling. Now all he had to do was find the appropriate costume and a date. Then he would meet the prince and let him know that there was no way in hell he was going to get Bethany. He had plans for her and her father's money.

Nicholas took their little talk better than she expected, especially when she introduced him to Armana the young woman from the boutique. The two of them hit it off and Nicholas even invited her to be his date for the costume party, which she accepted. The older archeologists were sitting this one out. They were still tired from their stay at the palace, and were looking forward to a little relaxation away from the media before the story broke about the discovery of the mummy. Bethany had chosen her costume and was pissed to discover that she had put on a couple of pounds since she arrived in Egypt. She blamed it on all the exotic dishes she had been eating, especially the tahini dip of which she'd grown extremely fond.

She didn't have a date for the event, but Nicholas agreed that she could be a third wheel in the limo with him and Armana. Feneas had agreed to be chauffeur again, which he didn't mind since he too would be attending the party with his girlfriend. Bethany didn't mind going stag…it wasn't as if she had not done it before.

All eyes were on her as she entered the party dressed as Cleopatra, the Queen of the Nile. The gown was gold, and it came complete with dark wig, crown, and scepter. Around her forearms, she wore asp shaped bracelets, with a red neckpiece around her throat. It matched the girdle around her waist. Both sides of the gown had slits that showed off a good bit of her legs. Nicholas gulped when he saw her. He was dressed as Caesar, and Armana was going to be a goddess. Armana didn't appear shocked to see her in the limousine. In fact, she was ready to tell Bethany about the new line of fashions that had just arrived that would be perfect for her.

"I really don't think I'll need any more party clothes since I'll probably be going home soon."

"But you must have something new for every event while you're dating the prince."

Bethany corrected her. "I am not dating the prince."

"Yes, you are," Nicholas replied. "The entire world knows it."

"I met the man once. That does not constitute dating."

Armana didn't agree. "But I've seen the pictures, and read the stories."

"Don't believe everything you read. The prince was just being polite."

"Darn, the two of you looked so good together."

"Okay, I'll tell you what. If this does become a relationship, I'll buy all the clothes from you exclusively."

Feneas' date was a lovely young woman with big brown eyes and short black hair. She could tell that he was taken with her by the way he held the door for her as she climbed into the limousine. She was dressed as an Egyptian temple priestess, while Feneas got a kick out of going as a soldier of Rome. They drove to the hotel where the party was being held. The theme was the meeting of Egypt and Rome, and there were a couple of Cleopatras, a few Marc Anthonys, and a couple of pharaohs. Feneas parked the car and the five of them walked into the ballroom. The place was decorated with columns and statues of long dead kings. The band was a popular rock group from the area, and people were dancing and having a good time from the moment they arrived. Several men winked at her as she walked by, but Bethany just smiled and ignored them.

"Isn't that Mark?" Bethany asked Nicholas who was deeply engrossed in a conversation with Armana.

Nicholas looked up. "Yes, it is. I wonder what he is doing here. And he has a date."

Apparently, he and Nicholas thought that fact would get a reaction out of her, but all she felt was sympathy for the young woman. Mark was dressed as a gladiator, while his date had chosen servant girl. He made it a point to seek them out and show the young woman off.

"Good evening, everyone."

"Hi, Mark," Bethany said. "What are you doing here?"

"The hotel invited me for rescuing you from that bandit and clearing them of neglect since you were staying here when you were taken."

"That was sweet of them. Who is your date?"

"This is Syria. She is a secretary. We just recently met and hit it off." He turned to his date. "Syria, this is Bethany Dailet and Nicholas Stewart, they're archeologist friends of mine. Bethany and I used to date."

"I know who she is," Syria replied happily. "She is the one dating our prince. Where is he? Is he here?"

Bethany smirked. She bet Mark didn't expect that reaction.

"Never mind," Mark said, steering her away from them. "Let's get something to eat. Later," he said to them and hurried off.

The food was a scrumptious meal of roasted lamb. There was non-alcoholic champagne, which Bethany stayed far away from. After dinner, the tables were cleared away again, and the couples took to the dance floor. Bethany wandered around talking with the people in the hotel, and mingling with the other celebrators. When she was bored with that she walked out to the front of the place and leaned against the railing.

"Didn't you learn anything the last time, Ms. Dailet?" a deep, familiar voice said.

Bethany quickly turned around. "Al-Shar?"

He bowed. "Sweet Bethany. Didn't you get in trouble the last time you wandered outside of this hotel?"

"What are you doing here?" She looked around. "It isn't safe. Mark is here."

"I'm safe. It's a costume party and I'm wearing a mask." He walked over to her. He was dressed as Pharaoh Ramesses. "Nice legs."

He pulled her into his arms. "Yours are better. I've missed you."

Bethany pushed away from him. "It's been over a month. You couldn't have missed me that much."

"As you said, it was not safe." He paused. "And you have been busy yourself. How is Prince Amasis?"

Bethany blushed. He knew.

"I do read."

"I guess he's fine."

"What do you mean, you guess? Aren't the two of you dating?"

"Why does everyone assume that? I've spent more time with you than with him."

"But he is every woman's fantasy. He's rich, famous and a snazzy dresser."

"Are you trying to sell me on him?"

He laughed. "Of course not. You are mine. I traded ten horses for you, remember?"

"How can I forget? You said that Maaches got the better end of the deal."

He cupped her jaw and ran his thumb across her bottom lip tenderly. "That was before we…." He stopped.

"Before we what? Go on and say it."

"Before we made love."

"Now, was that so hard to say?"

He lowered his lips to hers, brushing the mask aside so that he could feel the full impact. He forced his tongue through her lips and savagely kissed her. Releasing her, he said, "Yes, it was hard because I don't remember it. I was so high from whatever Khalaf had in that damn water pipe that I missed out what was probably the best night of my life."

Bethany giggled. "I don't remember either. All I had to remind me were the hickies and very tender breasts."

He released her. "We can remedy that. We can go someplace."

"I'm here with others. They would miss me." *Now why didn't I just say no?*

"Make up an excuse to leave for about an hour."

"I can't do that. They'll get suspicious."

"Don't you want to find out what you've missed? I want to make you come, screaming my name."

It was tempting. "What can I tell them?"

"Tell them that you are going for a ride with the prince, and he's going to drop you back off at your bungalow."

"How do you know that I am staying at a bungalow?" She shook her head. "Never mind. You want me to lie? What if Yahi shows up here?"

"He won't," Al-Shar assured her. "He is out of town?"

"You're pretty sure of yourself."

He swatted her on her butt. "I'm already rock hard. Do you want to feel?"

Bethany reached inside her gold clutch and took out her cell phone. She dialed Nicholas and explained the situation to him and then she hung up before he could argue. "Let's go," she ordered. "And you better be as good as every woman I've met thinks you are."

CHAPTER 16

S he was kind of expecting to see Midnight, but instead he led her to a fancy black sports car, complete with chrome hubcaps.

"Who did you steal this from?" she asked as she slid onto the leather seat. Al-Shar just laughed and closed the door for her. He ran around, slid in behind the wheel and sped out of the parking lot before Nicholas or anyone else could come out to investigate. "Where are we going?"

"I have a place nearby. It is private and no one will disturb us."

The sports car flew down the highway, and then he suddenly turned down a dark road. Moments later he drove down a gravel road, and then up to a set of gates that he had to use a security code to enter. A gorgeous mansion appeared. The palace was dark and far away from the highway. He drove the car into a garage, which he opened first with a remote. Al-Shar climbed out and opened the door for her. "Whose place is this?"

Al-Shar turned on a light and they stood in a formal foyer. "Mine, I told you." He took her through quickly, switching on the lights and switching them back off again as they passed through rooms with magnificently expensive furniture and art.

"How can a thief afford all of this?"

"I have told you countless times that I am not a thief."

"Then what are you?" she asked as he flipped the lights on in what had to be a master bedroom. The placed smelled like the cologne he wore.

"A man desperate to make love to you." He spun her around and slid the zipper down the back of her costume, exposing her bare back. She didn't have on a bra, just a thong that matched her costume. She felt his lips press against her neck and then he worked his way down to the small of her back. Bethany shivered as she stepped from the costume. Al-Shar's lips were magical. He spun her around to face him. She watched him as he sought out her breasts and suckled at them. Bethany rested against the footboard of the bed, arching her back and pushing her chest out to him. His touch was rough, but not calloused. He wore a gold ring and the cool metal made her nipples rise.

"Um," he said as he sucked. "These breasts will nurse many fine sons."

Her head went back. "Do you like children?"

"I love them," he answered as he switched nipples. "I want a harem full."

Her head snapped back up. "What did you say?"

"Nothing." He dropped down to his knees and kissed his way down her stomach. Bethany took air in her lungs as he used his tongue to seek out her navel. He toyed with the thong for a moment and then he rose, swept her up in his arms, and placed her on the bed. "I need to see the rest of you," he said as he slid the thong down her hips, thighs, and long legs. The only things remaining were her high heels. "These will have to go too. I want you the way you came into the world."

Bethany snatched the wig from her head undid her hair and shook it free. Al-Shar growled, approached, got down on his knees, and spread her legs. "You are shaven."

"Yes, the hair itches."

He buried his face between her legs, found her vagina, and pushed his tongue in. She wiggled as he got into what he was doing. *He has to move the mask aside to do that*, she thought as she tried not to moan. She tried to sit up to see, but he gently pushed her back down. "Relax," he replied. "The night is still young."

Bethany relaxed and gave up on seeing his face for the moment. Al-Shar raised her legs, exposing all of her to him. She supposed she should have been embarrassed by what he was doing, but all it did was take her inhibitions away.

"Oh," she moaned as he introduced a finger inside of her. She was so sensitive that she even felt when he pushed his knuckle in. He pulled it out slowly and then put in two fingers the next time and moved them around to stir up her juices. "Your fingers are so thick, ooh." He also had a beard, which rubbed against her delicate skin. Well, at least that was a little more that she knew about him.

Al-Shar quickly removed them. "Not yet, my love." He went back to working her with his mouth, and then out of the blue he eased his finger into her rectum.

"Oh!" she gasped. Bethany bit her lip as he worked both her holes at the same time. "That's interesting." She expected it to hurt, but it didn't. The two sensations nearly took her breath away and it felt so good. "Oh, oh, oh." Her body trembled.

"That's it, my princess," he said as he worked his finger in deeper. "Come for me." He put his mouth on her clitoris and rubbed hard.

Bethany didn't need much encouragement. Her vaginal walls opened and she erupted. Her stomach muscles tightened as spasms ripped through her. She gushed like a geyser. Al-Shar removed his fingers and wiped his lips. "I think you are ready."

Bethany sat up after she recovered. Al-Shar lowered the lights and began to strip out of his costume. She lay back down and rolled over on her side to get a better look. The costume dropped to the floor, followed by the tunic. He stood before her in a pair of mesh briefs, his hood, the mask and sandals. She eyed his chest hungrily. It was muscled and well-toned. And his abs rippled. Just the sight turned her on again. She allowed her eyes to wander down to the briefs. His penis moved against the fabric. He was big, even in a semi-erect state. Al-Shar moved it just to let her know he understood. He kicked out of the sandals, and removed the hood. Bethany groaned disappointedly once she discovered that she still couldn't see his hair because it was tightly bound beneath a do-rag. "You're horrible," she said as he approached. "I thought I was going to at least see your hair."

"Yes, I am, but you already knew that."

"You're not going to let me see your face, are you?"

"Not this time." He ran his hand down to the briefs. "But I'm about to show you something much more interesting." He slowly slid the briefs down his hips.

Bethany eyes widened. "I'm certainly impressed." He was shaven too. She smirked. He had taken away the evidence that would have at least told her his true hair color. There wasn't a speck of hair on him showing; even his eyebrows were always hidden. She thought his eyelashes could probably be brown, but she wasn't sure. She slid to the end of the bed and touched him. He was hard, but not fully erect yet. She lowered her head, but he stopped her. "Tonight is only about you, my love."

Bethany stepped off the bed and dropped to her knees before him. "Don't be selfish, Al. I want to taste you."

His eyes nearly rolled back in his head as she slid her tongue around the head of his penis like a snake, flicking her tongue, making it dance up the base and around the balls. He gripped the bedpost because his knees weakened as she watched her work on him. He moved his eyes away and they landed on that fantastic rump of hers. Too bad it was facing the other way because his palms itched to strike the cheek until it turned red. Bethany engulfed the head and slid him into her mouth. The feeling was indescribable. She moved her head down suddenly and deep-throated him.

"Ah," he moaned. "You are going to make me come prematurely." Bethany chuckled her way back to the tip where she applied pressure around the head. She released him and then took him in her hand and jacked him off. The tissues were so sensitive that he shuddered with each pump of her hand. His knees shook. *I have to stop her.* "Enough," he said. "You're going to make it go off."

Bethany removed her hands and smiled up at him. His heart skipped a couple of beats. He swept her up into his arms and put her back onto his bed. He followed, crawling between her satiny thighs.

"At least remove the mask," she begged.

He clapped his hands and extinguished the lights. "Nice try. He spread her legs apart. "But no." He entered her. "Ah."

Her breathing came in shallow gasps as he made love to her. She got wet quickly and soon he was sliding in and out of her with a rhythm. "Are you okay?" It was dark and he could not see if she was enjoying herself or not.

"Um hum," she purred. "I'm fine. You fill me completely."

His spirits soared and he continued to pump into her. Bethany wrapped her legs around his hips and pulled him down on her. His mouth captured hers for a kiss. "I'm so sorry I don't remember our first time together. I wonder if it was as good as it is now?"

"I hope so," she said kissing him back. She gasped, "Deeper."

Al chuckled. He raised her hips slightly and went in deeper. Bethany shivered and moaned louder. She was close to erupting again. He could tell by the way she moved beneath him. She nipped at his chest with his teeth and tongued one of his nipples. She was ready. Al slid off of her, got to his knees, raised her hips and slowly withdrew his penis until only the head remained inside of her. Bethany gasped and then he plunged back in.

"Oh," she whispered hoarsely. "I think you hit an ovary."

He chuckled withdrew again and then slammed into her, this time going in deeper.

"I'm so close."

"Work with me, Bethany. Roll that lovely ass of yours."

Bethany rotated her hips and he slid out again and pushed into her. He felt her open up. This time he ground his pelvis against her clitoris. Bethany clutched his back with her nails. "Oh."

"Not loud enough for me. You have to sing my name." He withdrew and changed places with her. "You have to work for it if you want it. Mount me and have your way with me."

Bethany pushed her damp hair from her face, sat down on him and engulfed him. "Ow," she moaned as she realized that he had been holding back on her. "You feel even larger this way."

He gripped her bottom, raised her up, and then moved her up and down on his shaft to show her how to do it to make it pleasurable for both of them.

"Oh, this feels so good." She got the rhythm and began to ride him softly at first and then with more vigor. After a while, all he could do was just lie there and let her enjoy herself. He kept time by massaging and squeezing the nipples of her breasts. "Oh, Oh," Bethany uttered as she bounced down hard on his jock once too much. "I think I'm about to come."

Al rejoined the action. He spread her open and used his arm muscles to move her back and forth quickly. She was so deliciously wet that she literally glided.

"Oh, Oh, Al-Shar," she screamed as the orgasm rocked her sweating body. She trembled, and her juices gushed out and flooded his thighs. He let her ride it out and waited for her to recover. "I don't think I can move," she said as she slid off his lap.

He flipped her over onto her knees and put a pillow under her hips. "You don't have to. I plan to do all the work now. He chuckled. "Damn woman, you released the Niagara Falls on me." He slapped her across the buttocks.

Bethany yelped. "Why did you do that?"

"Because you've been very naughty, Ms. Dailet." He struck her again and then massaged the spot.

"Ow, Yummy. How was I naughty?"

He bent over and kissed the cheek. "You argued with me, you've been hard-headed and had left the party with a masked man, and you have been fraternizing with an archeologist geek who loves you." He slapped the other cheek. "And your fiancé."

Bethany groaned and wiggled. "Not my fault, dear bandit. I can't help it if they like me. Is that all?"

He slapped her cheek again. "No, this is for canoodling with the royal whelp."

"Oh, canoodling? What the hell is that?" She giggled. "He was charming and he let me see his face. I'm sorry for being a desirable woman in the eyes of men, dear Pharaoh."

He popped her again. "What was that for?"

"For coming into my life, disrupting my plans and for making me feel something I've never felt before."

Bethany lifted her head. "Really?"

"Yes. You have stolen my heart, Bethany." He spread the cheeks and rubbed his penis against her anus.

She shivered. "I'm not sorry for that. I thought you hated me."

"Oh, no," he said as a tiny thread of his semen came out of the tip of his penis. He used it to slide up and down her crevice. "I would love to take you this way."

"Do it," she said. "I'm not afraid."

"No, there's not enough time." He felt dizzy. He moved his penis down. It jumped in his hands. He parted the lips of her vagina and entered her. "Oh." He rose over her buttocks and took her doggy-style. Bethany's head thrashed as he plunged into her already sensitive hole. She rolled her hips against the pillow between her legs to keep the juices flowing.

"How is it possible after two orgasms that I still want you so desperately?"

His heartbeat slowed. "I don't know." His legs strained to keep from coming. He withdrew slowly and then eased back in. His knees shook and his toes tingled. "I want you to come with me, Bethany. Do you think you can do it? I am so close and struggling to wait for you."

"Yes."

"Flip over on your back quickly," Al ordered as the fever rose in him. "I want to see those blue eyes when I come." He withdrew and Bethany flipped over on her back and exposed herself to him. Even in the dark, he could make out the tiny pink fold.

"I want you to bury yourself so deep inside me that we are one, Al."

"Yes, my love," he said as he spread her legs apart with his knees. His penis jumped. "Are you ready?"

"Yes, hurry," she pleaded.

"This may hurt a bit." He entered her roughly and plunged deep. "Ah," he grunted as the blood left his brain and went down to his penis. His hips moved furiously as he took her. Bethany humped with him.

"I'm coming," she screamed. "Al!"

"Me too, darling. It's a gusher." The semen shot from him like a nuclear missile, cramping his stomach and curling his toes. "Ouch," he said as he emptied himself. "That feels fatal." His penis continued to shoot even though the flow had stopped.

Bethany clung to him as she too, climaxed. Her fingernails scratched his back and her vagina throbbed.

He fell on her pressing her down with his weight. "I will kill any man who touches you," he promised as the last shudder left his body. He lowered his lips to hers. She sighed contently beneath him.

"You don't have to worry about that. You've branded me."

He rolled off her so that they both could breathe. Something ran through his head. He clapped his hands and the lights turned on. "I know this is a bad time to ask, but are you on the pill?"

Bethany sat up, pulled the pillow from behind her head and hit him with it. "Yes, it's a bad time to ask, but no. I'm not on the pill."

"Loop? Patch? Female condom?"

"No, no, no."

"Why not?"

"Because I wasn't sexually active until I met you."

"But you're engaged to Kauffman." He rose up on an elbow and fingered a nipple that was still swollen. Her breasts were huge and full.

Bethany slapped his hand away. "How many times do I have to tell you that Mark and I are not engaged? We've had sex twice, and both times were disastrous. I just gave up on him and it didn't make sense to spend the money on contraceptives I wasn't going to need."

"So you're telling me that me that I'm the only man you've been with since then?"

"Yes, what about you?"

"What about me?" He hefted one of her breasts. It felt warm.

"Am I the only woman you've been with this week?"

He laughed and removed his hand. "I can honestly say, yes."

"Good, end of conversation."

"I don't think so. We just made unprotected love."

Bethany rose and stepped from the bed. "Don't worry about it. I haven't had a period in almost two months now. I think it stopped because of all the heat and all the mountain and tomb climbing I've been doing." She walked into the bathroom, turned on the light and screamed. "You have a sunken tub, you rat. You know I love sunken tubs. I'm going in."

Al chuckled. "You go right ahead. Knock yourself out. There's bubble bath beneath the counter."

Bethany closed the door and turned on the tub.

Al rolled over on his back and pulled the covers up to his waist. No period for two months? That would be around the time of Emir's party. He looked toward the bathroom door. Bethany was giggling and splashing in the tub. *Hum, this could be a very sticky situation.*

Mark dropped his date off and headed back toward his hotel, still upset by what he had witnessed earlier…his meal ticket leaving the party with some other man…a prince. Well that was about to change. He hadn't come all the way to Egypt just to lose out on the Dailet fortune. He had to find a way to win her back. Then they could get married. That was the first part of the plan. The second part was to have someone kill her shortly after the honeymoon so he could not only collect on the sizeable insurance policy that he planned to take out on her, but also get her share of her inheritance from her family. He entered the hotel room and removed his costume. He bet if he really tried hard that he could find someone in Egypt who wouldn't have a problem killing her. Maaches and Sabola probably would have done it for little or no money, but they had disappeared off the face of the earth. The bandit Al-Shar probably had them killed and buried them in the desert where no one could find them. But he wasn't worried about that now. He found those two just days after arriving in Egypt and he was sure that he could find a hit man in no time.

He took a quick shower and climbed into bed. "Now how am I going to woo her away from the prince?" He snapped his fingers. He'd start by bringing her flowers and pretending to be interested in her work. She was always a sucker for sweet talk. Maybe he would find Al-Shar Khan and turn him into the law. Then she might be grateful enough. No, Al-Shar was too smart and had too many contacts. *Hey wait*. He wondered if Al-Shar would be interested in bumping Bethany off. He couldn't be charged with kidnapping and slave-trading if the victim suddenly disappeared. "That's it. I will seek out Al-Shar and make him a very generous offer."

The next night he walked into the same bar where he had met Maaches and Sabola and started asking around for the bandit.

"I know him," a woman replied as she did a lap dance for a man next to his table.

"I need to get in touch with him. It is very important."

"I can take a message to him for a price."

Mark grinned. "Name your price."

CHAPTER 17

"*W*hen are you ever going to get some work done?" Andre asked Bethany as she read out loud an invitation from Prince Amasis to come to the palace for a couple of days."

Bethany shrugged her shoulders. "Most of my work is done. It's up to those tomb-geek guys to positively identify the mummy."

"No, I mean the other work. Or, have you forgotten the real reason we are here."

"No, I've taken enough soil samples and I've been analyzing them in my spare time. Anyway, we can't go digging at the site anymore. Hathor's people have the area barricaded off until all the tunnels have been cleared."

"So, are you thinking about accepting the prince's invitation?"

"I'm thinking about it. He wants me to stay for a couple of days, but I don't know."

"You'll never get a chance like this again. There are no princes in Indianapolis."

"I know," Bethany replied. She was only considered going so she could put an end to whatever relationship he thought they had. There was no way she could be with him after spending time with Al-Shar. She figured the best thing for her to do was to go back to the United States and wash both of them out of her system. She sighed. That was starting to be her full-time job.

First Mark, then Nicholas, and now Yahi. "As tempting as it all sounds, I do have a life back home."

"You can have that life here."

"Are you trying to get rid of me?"

"No, I'm just saying that don't let a job keep you from finding love."

That wasn't a problem. She was in love with Al-Shar. She realized it the moment she saw him again. Yes, she was going to accept the prince's invitation and tell him that she was going back home to the United States. "I better go pack," she said, sliding off the chair. "I think he's sending a limousine for me."

"I'll see you when you get back. Try to make the right decision."

"I didn't know you could play chess," Bethany said to Yahi later that day.

"He cheats," Jamaal replied as he concentrated on the board.

"I do not cheat. You are just jealous because you have yet to beat me." He moved his piece, capturing Jamaal's.

"Ah, man I didn't see that. I was distracted."

"That is an excuse." Yahi moved again and won the game.

"Damn," Jamaal said. "I guess it's time for me to give up and go find Kasia."

"The two of you still dating?" Bethany asked.

"Yes," Jamaal answered. "I am wearing her down. I know any day now she will be professing her love for me."

Yahi laughed. "Don't hold your breath."

"You wound me, Yahi. I thought I was your best friend."

"You are, but you can't wear Kasia down. You have to deal with her on her level. You, my friend, must go shopping with her."

"I'm rich, Yahi, but I don't think I'm that rich."

Yahi chuckled. "She has a black credit card. She has no limit."

Jamaal rose, leaving the two of them together.

"Do you play?" Yahi asked.

"No."

"Would you like to learn?"

"Yes."

Yahi reset the board. Hours later, she had the gist of the game, but she didn't really like it. She thought it would be like checkers. "It's an acquired taste," he told her. "We have to stop anyway. We are going out to dinner tonight."

"Out?" Bethany asked.

"Yes, on a date. We are going out on the town. I have made reservations."

"But I didn't bring anything fancy to wear."

"Don't worry. I have taken care of all of that. I have ordered something from your friend Armana."

"How do you know that she's my friend?"

"Have you forgotten that I am a prince? I have contacts."

"You have spies, you mean?"

"Exactly. You have a passion for bright things. I have chosen the perfect dress. It is in your room."

Bethany walked with him to the stairs. "Are you always so forward?"

"Yes. It's the only way to get things done."

He had made reservations for them at the top of the Cairo Towers. They were alone except for the bodyguards who stayed out of their way watching the doors to make sure no one except the restaurant workers entered. The atmosphere was romantic. Someone had decorated with flowers and hanging plants and the music was soft and soul searching. Her date looked dashing in his white suit and he was saying all the right things, making it difficult for her to tell him what she planned to tell him.

After dinner, he took her into his arms and they slow danced to the music. Her body responded to his touch and his kisses, but deep down she felt lousy for betraying Al-Shar. There was non-alcoholic champagne chilling in an ice bucket when they returned to the table. Bethany eyed it with dread. Yahi popped the cork, filled two glasses and handed one to her. "I don't think I should. Champagne makes me a bit silly."

"Just one glass," he coaxed. "To help you relax, and besides it's not the real thing."

Foolishly, she accepted the glass.

"It is okay to get a little silly sometimes."

He entertained her with stories of his youth, capturing her attention as he told her tales of racing camels across the Sahara and spending many nights on a boat on the Nile River. It all sounded so glamorous and exciting that the words refused to come out about her leaving. So she had a little more champagne and a little more dancing. Dessert arrived and consisted of strawberries and hot chocolate sauce which Yahi dipped and fed to her. His tongue slid over her bottom lip to remove the chocolate residue left behind by their clumsiness. The next thing she knew she was downstairs in a hotel room alone with him wondering how she was going to get herself out of the situation she was in. She felt like a wanton for desiring him so soon after being with Al-Shar. She convinced herself that it was just sex. That no one else had to know. She was out of the beautiful silk dress before she knew it and trembling beneath his powerful princely thrusts. The orgasms kept coming as he took her in every position possible. His touch was gentle as he explored every inch of her body and just when she thought she couldn't take any more he brought her to one mind-blowing orgasm before coming deep inside of her.

"You are magnificent," he said as he held her in his arms afterwards. "Please never leave me."

Bethany lay awake long after he dozed off. *What am I going to do? Is it possible to be in love with two men at the same time?* She knew the answer already. Yahi, with all his honesty, had crept into her heart.

Kasia came out of the bathhouse clutching a terrycloth robe around her, while Jamaal waited on a lawn chair beside the pool. "Don't be shy," he told her. "Does the suit fit?"

Kasia sat down on a chair on the opposite side of the table. "Yes."

"Well aren't you going to show it to me?" She was a striking brunette with big brown eyes and he had been in love with her forever.

"I'm nearly naked."

"Are you blushing?" he asked as he got out of his seat and walked over to her. "No need to. I don't want you to feel uncomfortable."

She rose, barely reaching his chest. "I'm not. I'm just afraid you might not like it after seeing your reaction to Ms. Dailet in her suit."

He chuckled. "I am sure that I won't be disappointed." He unbuttoned the robe and helped her out of it. He looked down and gulped. Kasia's breasts rose and fell in the skimpy red bra that barely covered her nipples. He stepped back to get the full effect. "You are simply exquisite." He pulled her into his arms.

"I guess this means that you approve."

He released her. "Very much." He escorted her back to the table. "We will dine first and then talk, and then maybe swim later."

Kasia nodded. "I'd like that."

He didn't ever remember her being so shy. Usually she talked nonstop about her tennis games or her clothes. Lately she had decided that she wanted to design clothes like Bethany's mother. In the last two days, the two women had struck up a wonderful friendship.

"What do you think of Bethany Dailet?" Kasia asked after they had finished their meal.

"She's a nice young woman. Very smart and level-headed. Yahi seems to like her a lot. Why?"

"I was just wondering. I think Yahi is in love with her."

"Would that be so bad?"

"No, I like her, and I think she will be good for him."

"You don't have a problem with her just being an American archeologist?"

"No, why should I. I don't judge people by money or titles."

"I'm glad to hear that." He reached into his pocket and pulled out a little black box and pushed it toward her.

"What is this?" Kasia asked.

"Open it."

Kasia slowly opened the box. "It's a ring."

Jamaal got out of his chair, walked over to her and went down on one knee. "Would you do me the honor of becoming my wife?"

Kasia squealed and flung herself into his arms, nearly knocking both of them into the pool. "Yes, Amizada Hatem."

Jamaal blushed. She had called him by his full title. He kissed her as she lay atop of him.

Someone cleared his throat to get their attention. "Get a room you two."

Jamaal looked up smiling. It was Yahi. "Nice suit, Sis. It fits that big ass of yours like a glove, doesn't it, Jamaal?"

Jamaal slid Kasia off his lap. "It certainly does."

Kasia flashed her ring at her brother.

"What is that?"

"An engagement ring. Jamaal has asked me to marry him."

Yahi helped Jamaal from the ground and grabbed him into his arms in a bear hug. "Congratulations. I'm so excited for the two of you."

Jamaal laughed. "You can free me now before Kasia gets the wrong idea."

Yahi freed him. He grabbed at his baby sister. "It's about time you put Jamaal out of his misery. He loves you so much."

"I love him too," she confessed. "Ever since I can remember he was always there, taking care of me and watching out for me."

"When are you going to tell the folks?"

"Later, after we change," Kasia replied. "I don't think father would appreciate seeing me in this suit."

"He'd skin me alive," Jamaal said nervously.

Yahi laughed. "That's because she's daddy's little girl."

"Speaking of daddy's little girl, where's Bethany?"

Yahi blushed. "She's in her room sleeping like a baby."

Kasia excused herself and went to the pool house to change.

"How was your night out?"

"The second best night of my life. We dined and danced, and then we…"

"No explanations needed," Jamaal assured him. "You're going to marry her, aren't you?"

"Yes," Yahi confessed. "She doesn't know it yet, but I think she's carrying my child."

"Huh? The two of you only got together last night."

"Yes, but she was with Al-Shar a couple of months ago at your father's palace. We were both very, very stoned, and she danced this very provocative belly dance that had every man there with a perpetual hard-on."

Jamaal gulped. "How and the hell are you going to fix this? Poor Bethany is probably very confused right about now. She's cheated on you with you."

"And she loves both of us."

"This is one of those times I'm glad I'm not in your shoes."

"Enough about me. You're going to be married. It shall be a big celebration. The joining of two of the noblest families on the African continent."

Jamaal flopped down on the chair. "I'm scared, Yahi. What if I'm not good in bed?"

"You were doing pretty well when I walked up, and I've never heard any of the ladies in the harem complain."

Jamaal blushed. "No, me either, but Kasia is different. She is a princess."

"They're still built the same. You'll know you've done well when she screams your name."

"You're horrible, Yahi."

Yahi laughed. "Yeah, so I've been told."

Jamila accepted the coin Al-Shar paid her for the information she had for him. The two of them had done business before. He really didn't like doing business with women, but she always provided him with the information he needed.

"A man wants to hire you to do a specific job for him. It's of a delicate nature if you know what I mean?"

"He wants me to kill someone?"

Jamila nodded. "And get rid of the evidence. Money is no object."

Al's insides fluttered. He had never harmed a living soul in his life, so why did anyone think he would start now. "Who is this person?"

Jamila passed him a note. "All the information is written on this."

Al opened it, read and nodded. He rose. "Thanks."

"Do you want me to alert the police?"

"No, I'll take care of it." He had worked stings with a couple of cops in his employ before. They would get this one too. He stepped out of the bar. It was late and he was tired. He drove back to his place in Luxor, made a couple of quick calls, and then climbed into bed. It was nights like these that he did not return to the palace. He couldn't jeopardize their safety in case he was followed. Hopefully, it would be the last time. He was growing tired of playing the bad guy and he hated the masks almost as much as Bethany did.

Thoughts of her filled his mind. Images of her in mid-coitus appeared as vividly now as it had when they were alone together. To think that someone despised her enough to want her dead filled him with such despair. He needed her at that very moment, but she was probably asleep at the bungalow. He rolled over and dialed her cell phone number hoping that she would not be annoyed at him for awakening her. But he needed to hear her voice, and needed to know that she was okay.

"Hello."

"Hello, sweet, Bethany."

"Al?"

"Yes, my darling. I know it's late, but I just needed to hear your voice."

"Are you okay?"

"Yes, I just couldn't sleep. I can't get you off my mind."

She giggled. "How sweet."

"I need to see you."

"When?"

"Now."

"Don't be silly. It's late and everyone is here."

"I don't care. I need to hold you in my arms and smell your clean scent."

She sighed. "You're making this real hard to say no."

"Then don't. I can be there within the hour. I will call when I'm near."

She never snuck a boy into her home before, so imagine trying to sneak a full-gown man into a bungalow at two o'clock in the morning. He crawled into her window, tore the gown from her body, and took her on the floor without making a sound. *Something is wrong*, she pondered as he slept fitfully beside her when they finally crawled into bed. Were the police after him again? Or was he being disturbed by something else? She looked over at him. He had his back to her. It still held old scratch marks as well as the fresh ones she had just given him as he pumped into her. She reached over and wrapped her arm around him. She missed him too. He made her feel safe, cherished and loved. It still frightened her that she knew almost nothing about him. She wasn't even sure if Al-Shar Khan was his real name. Was he so hideous underneath that mask that he thought that she would not want him anymore? She had no answers. She still couldn't figure out why Yahi also made her feel so cherished. The two of them were as different as night and day. Al-Shar could be mean and diabolical and a bit of a wild man, while Yahi was fun, refined and a romantic. Maybe that's why she liked both of them. It was like having a variety pack. She sighed. *Why couldn't it be just one man with all those qualities combined?*

Al-Shar stirred and turned to face her. "I have to go," he told her. "Before the others awaken."

Bethany nodded. "I understand." She kissed him. "Why are you so sad?"

"It's a long story. One that I hope will have a happy ending."

"Are you in trouble?"

"No, it's not me this time, but a friend. His life is in danger."

Bethany gasped.

Al-Shar put his finger to her lips to silence her. "I'm sorry that I was so rough with you earlier."

"It's okay. You make me cum when you go hard and deep. I think you've ruined me."

He chuckled. "I love you, Bethany."

"I love you too, Al-Shar." There, she had admitted it to him.

"Do you really, or do you love the way I make you feel when I make love to you?"

"Both. I don't know what I will do without you in my life."

"You have to go back to the United States soon?"

She put her finger to his lips. "Let's not discuss that now. You'll make me cry and I'll wake everyone up."

Al rose and struggled back into his clothes. "We'll figure out a way to work this out." He climbed out of the window and disappeared into the darkness.

CHAPTER 18

*A*l was almost to his car when he heard the barrel of a gun click behind him. He stopped in his tracks and turned. It was the older archeologist, George Eisemann, and he was holding the gun with some expertise.

"Don't move, or I'll blow your head off."

Al stopped. There was no doubt that he could get to the old guy before he could pull the trigger but something inside of him told him not to bother.

"Who are you?" George asked as he approached. "And what are you doing here?"

"My name is Al-Shar Khan."

George raised the gun higher. "The bandit?"

"Only Ms. Dailet calls me that."

"What are you doing here?"

"I came to check on Bethany and to make sure that she is okay."

"What do you mean?"

"I have to show you something. It is in my top pocket. Don't pull the trigger. I am unarmed." He reached into his pocket and extracted a piece of paper and held it out to George.

George opened it cautiously and read it.

"Do you know who that is?"

George nodded. "Why?"

"He has put a bounty on Bethany's head. He wants me to kill her."

George gasped. "Is that why you're here?"

"No, like I said before. I came to make sure that she was okay. I was a fool to let him bring her back here. I should have brought her back myself when I got her away from her kidnappers."

George lowered the gun. "I think I believe you. I don't know why. Maybe because I suspected that Kauffman might be up to something."

"I think he also murdered Bethany's father."

George nodded. "I do, too. I think he's after Bethany's money." He put the gun away. "What are we going to do?"

"I have a plan. I know Bethany thinks very highly of you, but I don't think she trusts me. I just want you to know that I would never do anything to harm her. In fact, I have foolishly fallen in love with her. She thinks that I am a thief and a bandit. It's not true. In fact, I'm just the opposite. But all this doesn't matter. Can I count on your cooperation?"

George nodded again.

"Good. I'm going to bring Mark Kauffman to justice. Just don't say anything to Bethany."

"I won't, but Mark is supposed to accompany us up to the tomb tomorrow. Prince Amasis and his people will be joining us too."

"The prince will not let anything happen to her. I will ask him to keep an eye on Kauffman too until I can take care of him."

"You know the prince?"

"Yes. He and I share common interests. I will keep in touch. Please don't repeat anything I have told you. Bethany's life depends on it."

Mark arrived just in time for breakfast the next morning. He was dressed in khaki shorts, and a short-sleeved shirt. And looking very much like the Mark she once knew and loved. He brought flowers and her favorite candy.

"Good morning, beautiful." He kissed her on the cheek.

"What's gotten into you?"

He pushed back a lock of blonde hair that escaped from her pony-tail.

"My heart just skipped a beat the moment I saw you in that Cleopatra costume the other night, and I was pretty pissed off with myself for having a date with someone who wasn't you."

Bethany let him in, accepted the flowers and candy and led him into the kitchen. "That part of our life is over."

"Yes, I know. But it can be rekindled. We had something special back then."

"You left me for another woman," she said as she fished around for a vase to put the flowers in.

"It was a mistake…a big one and I know I have done some pretty rotten things, but I've changed."

"Why?"

"Why what?"

"Why have you changed?"

"I don't know. I think it had to do with hearing about your disappearance. All I know is that I had to do something to find you. It tore me apart to think that you were dead."

"Would you like some breakfast? We have plenty."

"Sure," he said. "You were always a good cook."

Bethany prepared the meal. Nausea rumbled in her stomach when she cracked open the first egg.

"Are you okay? You looked a bit ill."

Bethany recovered quickly. "I'm okay. It's just this heat." She finished the eggs and brushed back the sweat from her brow. "I never thought I'd miss the snow back home."

"Yes, this heat is unbearable, but you seem to be thriving. Your skin is rosy and you look radiant."

Such sweet words. I wonder what he's up to. She prepared the meat and the toast. George, Andre and Nicholas joined them a few minutes later.

"I can't wait to see the tomb," Nicholas said. "Have they cleared it all out yet?"

"Not yet," George answered. "There are still several chambers left to explore. That's what we're going to do today."

"Good. I've always wanted to be a part of something historical."

They finished their breakfast and Feneas arrived. They climbed into the

SUV and went to the site. A long white limousine was there when they arrived.

"Who is that?" Mark asked.

Prince Yahi Amasis and his friend Jamaal stepped out.

Recognition registered on Mark's face. "What are they doing here?"

"I invited them," Bethany replied. "Like you, they have a sudden interest in history."

She didn't think Yahi could look so good in casual clothes, but she was wrong. Tight khaki pants, a short-sleeved tee shirt and tennis shoes took a whole new meaning on his tall muscular frame. Jamaal was similarly dressed but he had on a long-sleeved shirt. Yahi's gorgeous blue eyes were hidden behind a pair of dark aviator glasses that he removed as he walked over to her and kissed her passionately.

"Cut that out you two," Nicholas replied as he walked past them with his gear. "Some of us have just eaten breakfast."

"Ignore him," Bethany replied. "He's always grouchy until he's had his second cup of coffee." Mark walked over to them. "Yahi, this is Mark Kauffman, a friend of mine from back home."

"The realtor," Yahi said. He shook Mark's hand. "Thank you for rescuing Bethany from that awful bandit. If it wasn't for you we might never have met."

"It was my pleasure. Bethany and I go way back." He slapped her on the butt and walked over to George and Andre by the hole.

"Why is he here?" Yahi asked as he and Jamaal walked over to the table to pick up their hard hats.

"He asked to go down. He wants to be a part of history."

"I don't trust him," Jamaal replied. "He has evil eyes."

Yahi laughed. "My sentiments exactly.

Yahi stared, quite overwhelmed at the ancient hieroglyphics inside the tomb. "I'm awed," he told Jamaal. "To think that something so wonderful has laid buried here untouched for centuries."

Jamaal nodded. "Did you see the plaque at the entrance? It bares your name."

"It also bares a curse that whoever opens it will die a horrible death." He chuckled. "Imagine people believing in such things way back then." They followed the others up the stairs and through several corridors before arriving in the burial chambers.

"We found the mummy back here," Bethany told them. "It has been removed but the stone coffin remains."

Yahi, Jamaal and Mark peeped inside the stone structure. "Where are the other chambers?" Mark asked.

Bethany pointed. "George and the others went that way."

Mark left and Jamaal followed him. Bethany was about to move but was overcome by a bout of dizziness. Yahi caught her. "Are you okay?"

"Yes, I just got a little dizzy." She reached for her water bottle, and then she sat down on the ground, putting her head between her legs until the dizziness and nausea passed.

"I think it might be too hot in here for you. Would you like me to take you back up to the surface?"

"No, I'm okay. I'm probably catching a cold or something."

"We can't have you getting sick."

She rose. "Come on. Let's go see what's in those other chambers."

Yahi followed her. They arrived just in time to see them open the next chamber. The glow from the gold artifacts was blinding.

"Look at all this stuff," Mark replied greedily. "It must be worth billions."

"It's priceless," Yahi replied. He walked in and picked up a scroll. It had the word Amasis on it. He handed it to George. "I'm afraid to open it. It might crumble."

"I'll take care of it. It might be the royal birth certificate."

Mark was on his knees rummaging through a chest of jewels like a kid in a candy store.

Jamaal and Yahi walked through another door. "It's another sarcophagus." George, Andre and Nicholas hurried over. Bethany was about to join them when she witnessed Mark pocketing a couple of jewels. *Once a snake always a snake.*

"Thank you for coming," Mark said to the man.

Al-Shar sat down and his bodyguards stood guarding the doors. "I heard you have a job for me."

"A proposition. I need you to take care of a little matter for me. I need someone removed."

"I understand. Who is it?"

"Bethany Dailet."

"You must be kidding? I thought the two of you were engaged?"

"We are, but she's suddenly inherited a lot of money by the accidental death of her father. And you know I want it."

"His death was an accident?"

"Yes. He slipped and hit his head on something."

"Then why don't you just ask her for it?"

"Because that's an unrealistic thing to ask and she won't give it up that easy. She wants to be married. Okay, so I'll marry her in a couple of days, and then you can kill her."

"You make it sound easy."

"She's just a woman. Push her off a cliff or something."

"It's going to cost you."

Mark reached into his pocket and pulled out some gold jewelry and some precious stones. "I can get my hands on much more."

Al pocketed the jewels. He handed Mark a phone number. "Call me once you marry her." He rose and walked out of the bar. Two other men joined Mark at the table.

"I need you to go treasure hunting for me."

Al made the appropriate phone calls, including one to the Supreme Council of Antiquities warning them to put tight security on the tomb. There was no way he was going to allow that lousy bastard to get his hands on his family's artifacts. He fingered the jewels in his pocket. He'd turn them over to George Eisemann tomorrow when they met. He would also call Bethany later to check on her. She didn't look so good the last time he saw her. Even he could tell that she was suffering from a horrible bout of morning sickness. He had to find a way to keep her far away from the tomb before she passed out from the heat. He wondered when her next period was due. There was no way she won't suspect something after missing it for three months. Maybe he'll suggest that she seek out medical attention if she ever got sick around him again.

Bethany crawled out of the bathroom and by some miracle made it back to her bed. She was supposed to go back to the tomb with the others but she feared she was going to sit this one out. She didn't know how much longer she could go on without seeking medical attention. Crackers weren't working anymore and she was afraid to take anything stronger. Someone knocked on the door. "Come in."

George entered. "Are you feeling any better?"

"No, I feel like crap. I think I have the flu."

He felt her forehead. "You don't have a fever."

"Then it must have been something I ate."

"Would you like for me to stay with you today?"

"No, I'm okay. I probably just need some rest."

He rose. "I'll call back later to check on you. We are planning to get the rest of the treasure out of the tomb before any more looters show up."

"Funny, how they just showed up out of the blue. Luckily you thought enough ahead to have some guards watching it."

"Yes, there's been a lot of looting of the tombs lately. I just had a feeling that I'd better protect our investment." He smiled at her and left.

Bethany hopped from the bed and made it to the bathroom just in time. One more minute and she would have had to clean the bed and the floor in her room. She brushed her teeth, gargled and climbed into the shower. Afterwards she climbed back into bed and went off to sleep.

Al-Shar looked down on her as she slept. George had left the back door unlocked for him and he promised he would keep an eye on her, especially since Mark should know by now that his plan for robbing the tombs didn't work. Her eyes opened.

"Al-Shar? What are you doing here?"

"Checking on you. I heard you weren't feeling well."

She sat up. "Who told you?"

"Does it matter? I'm trying to do a good thing here."

"Go. I might be contagious."

"No. I'm not going to leave you. You need to eat something."

She buried herself back under the covers. "No way. I'm tired of throwing my guts up."

"Poor baby. Maybe you need to see a doctor."

"No doctor."

"Why not?" She didn't answer. "Okay, suit yourself."

She pushed the covers aside and dashed into the bathroom.

Al chuckled. She was so stubborn. He followed her. Nothing came up, but her body was rocked by dry heaves. He picked her up into his arms and carried her back to bed. He tucked her in. "I'll be back." Moments later he returned with a steaming bowl of soup, some crackers and some clear soda.

Bethany opened her eyes again. "What is all of this?"

"Food. You need to build up your strength."

"I can't keep it down, Al. Maybe I'm dying."

"No, you are not. Sit up and I'll feed you."

Bethany sat up and her gown slipped down at the collar exposing the tops of her breasts. He put some soup into her mouth and she swallowed. The action made her boobs jiggle. They were filling with milk already. His body hardened with fatherly pride and a little bit of lust. He continued to feed her until it was all gone. "The crackers and soda is for later in case you feel sick again."

She snuggled beneath the covers and he tucked them back under her chin. He brushed her hair away from her eyes and kissed her on the forehead. "You're so good to me," she muttered as sleep overtook her.

"That's because I love you, Bethany. I would do anything for you."

Al-Shar was gone by the time the others returned and she felt so much better. Bethany crawled out of the bed and went out to check the mail. There was a letter from the prince inviting her to join him for dinner. She didn't think it was wise for her to meet him and possibly contaminate him, but she hadn't seen him in a couple of days and they still needed to have that talk. She dressed and got Feneas to drive her into town to the restaurant on the note. She was quite surprised to find Mark there and not Yahi.

"You've arrived," Mark said as the waiter showed her over to the table. He got up and helped her into a seat.

"What are you doing here?"

"Didn't you get my invitation?"

"No, I got an invitation from the prince."

"Well, I didn't think you would have come if I had invited you."

"Maybe I might have. It would help if you could be honest and stop trying to con me."

"Okay, I understand." The waiter brought over their meal. "I took the liberty and ordered before you arrived. "I know you like fish."

"Thank you," Bethany said. She hoped she could keep it down. "You remembered."

"I remember a lot of things. We used to be so good together."

Bethany ate her fish. It was the first real food in her stomach besides soup in days and she hoped it would stay down with all the bull Mark was feeding her. "Things change, people change."

"But not my feelings for you. I know what you're thinking. I know I let money influence me in the past, and I was foolish. I never should have run out on you."

"No, you should not have." *Okay, what is he up to?*

"I think Egypt agrees with you. Your skin is glowing, and you've put on a little weight. I think it looks good on you."

"Thanks."

"I'm serious. You've always been beautiful. I just let other things get in the way."

Yep, Bethany thought. *He's up to something.*

Mark reached into his pocket, pulled out a brown box and handed it to her. Bethany opened it. There was a huge diamond engagement ring. She wondered how he could afford something like this. He probably hocked the jewels he swiped from the tomb.

"Will you marry me, Bethany? I promise that I will change. Say yes, and we can leave this place. We'll go back to Indianapolis and start all over again."

Bethany continued to look down at the ring. A year ago, she would have told him yes before the proposal left his mouth. But she was no longer in love with him. Her heart was now split between two men, so there was no way Mark had a chance.

"You don't have to answer yet. I don't want to rush you."

The ring certainly was pretty and she would be going home in a couple of weeks. *What to do? What to do?*

Mark took the decision away from her. Their engagement and upcoming marriage was posted as headlines the next morning in American newspapers.

"I think her head is about to explode," Nicholas said as he watched her read the article he gave her.

Andre agreed. "She looks like she is going to kill someone."

"I am," Bethany said. She stalked over to the phone and dialed the newspaper. "This is Bethany Dailet. I want a retraction published in tomorrow's newspaper. I am not engaged and I am not going to marry Mark Kauffman. The story is not true, and it has hurt a lot of people."

"But our sources are reliable. Mr. Kauffman gave us the story himself."

"I don't care. It's not true."

"I'm glad," the reporter on the other line said. "We've got a bet going that you're going to marry Prince Amasis within the month."

"Ah!" Bethany shouted. "Retract the story tomorrow." She hung up the phone, nearly cracking the base and walked away. The telephone rang and George answered it as he entered the dining room.

"Yes, she's here." He walked the phone over to her.

"Hello. Yes. No, it's not true. Yes, I'm sure. Okay." She hung up.

"Who was that?" Nicholas asked.

"King Waheed."

"What? The king called you personally? What did he want?"

"To find out if the story in the newspaper was true. Apparently, Yahi is heartbroken and has gone into seclusion."

"You broke the prince's heart," Nicholas teased.

"I did not. Sometimes men can be big old drama queens." She stormed out of the room to put on some clothes. It was bad enough that her period was late again, and now this engagement thing was going to drive her crazy.

"I can't believe the man would do something like this," Jamaal said to Yahi as they lounged around the pool.

"I can. It's part of his plot to marry her and then kill her."

"Your parents were quite upset."

"Well, I can't tell them the truth. At least not yet."

"What about the baby?"

"Bethany has been suffering from morning sickness. She thinks she has the flu."

"When is she going to the doctor?"

Yahi shrugged his shoulders. "I think she's afraid. I think she already suspects that she's pregnant and she's confused by who the baby's father is."

"That's your fault, Yahi."

"Yeah, I know. I just look at it as getting twice the sex."

"That baby is going to be rotten."

"To the core. I plan to spoil him."

"Well, whose turn is it this time?"

"I suppose it's mine, but I'm in seclusion, sulking and devastated by the wedding announcement."

"Al-Shar?"

Yahi nodded. "She needs a little tough love in her life right now. And besides, I haven't heard her scream my name in a while. Prince Yahi is a tender lover. He might get offended by her wanton ways, while Al-Shar loves it."

"You're one sick little puppy."

"Yeah, I know. She seems to like his home. I think I'll take her there tonight and feed my son."

"Yuck."

"Just wait. Your turn will come soon enough."

CHAPTER 19

"*H*ow did you get away?" Al asked Bethany as she stepped inside his home.

"I told the truth. I told them I was going to spend the night at a spa to get away from the media. I told them that I needed to rest."

"So you lied."

"You're rubbing off on me." She carried her small suitcase into the bedroom. "Anyway, it's not a complete lie. I can soak in the tub and get revitalized."

"It's waiting for us."

Bethany smirked. "You're going to join me?"

He nodded. "And then we'll do other things." He led her into the bathroom, removed his clothes, and stepped into the deep tub of bubbles. He waited for her to undress. She unbuttoned the sundress she had on and stood before him in her underwear. She turned toward the mirror, pulled her hair up, and secured it to the top of her head with a comb. She then unsnapped her bra with her back to him, allowing him a moment to gaze at her behind. She turned to face him. Her breasts were full and firm. His eyes dipped lower. There was a slight bump just below the navel. She slid out of the panties and climbed in.

"This feels good," she said as he washed her back. He took the comb from her hair and it cascaded down, nearly landing in the water. It had grown longer and thicker. "What are you doing?"

"I want to wash it."

"Do you know how?"

He laughed. "You slay me, Bethany Ann Dailet."

"Ooh, you know my full name." She leaned back and allowed him to wash her hair. He gently massaged her scalp, and then rinsed it out. He chose a fruity conditioner and repeated the action, and then he reached for a comb and pinned the hair back up so it could dry.

"Thanks, you did well," she teased. "I will recommend you to my friends."

"Come here," he said pulling her to him. "I want to hold you." He was already erect, and his penis bobbed against her stomach.

Bethany wiggled out of his grasp, grabbed the soap and the towel and began to wash himself from the neck down. She grabbed his penis and squeezed.

"I will come if your hands don't stop that."

She giggled, soaped it up and then rinsed him off. "Turn around and let me get your back."

He turned. "Some vile woman has marked you with her claws."

"Yes, she is a ferocious little minx. I will make her pay later."

Bethany tried to mount him, but the water made his phallus pop back out of her.

"Ooh, you're anxious." He went down and kissed her breast. The nipple hardened and the areola budded to the size of a silver dollar. He wondered how much larger they would grow in the next six months. He stroked it with his hand and Bethany whimpered.

"They are so sensitive. I can barely keep a bra on them."

He kissed both of them. "Poor baby. Maybe you should get bigger bras or go braless."

"Bigger bras, yes. Braless, no. I would have to beat those three guys at the bungalow off with sticks."

He chuckled. "Even George?"

"Yes, he's still a man."

"Let's get out of the water before we start to prune."

He got towels, while Bethany climbed out. He watched her out of the corner of his eyes just in case she slipped. They dried off and raced to the bed like a couple of kids. Bethany climbed on first. Al gulped as he watched. *What an ass.* He grew erect. *Could I? No, it would never fit.* He walked over toward the bed. He knew that the first trimester was a crucial time in any pregnancy so he had told himself not to get too rough with her even if she begged. "Are you sure you're feeling up to it?"

Bethany spread her legs. "I think so."

Their lovemaking started out slow, just a little foreplay to get her wet and then he mounted her, sinking into her warm crevice. It had changed. She seemed tighter, like nature had put up a defense to protect the baby. He raised her thighs and worked it in slowly. He strummed her clitoris as he deep stroked her. Through all of it she kept her eyes closed and smiled. She went off without warning, soaking his fingers.

"It just snuck up on me," she said with an impish grin. "Everything down there feels so different. My nerves are so sensitive. I felt like I was about to come the moment you entered me."

"I've noticed a difference too. You're tighter. Maybe there is something in the water."

She sat up and ran her hand up and down his chest and abs. "Your body was sculptured by the gods," she replied, eyeing him hungrily. She pushed him down on his back and ran her tongue around his nipples, chest and down his stomach. Al winced as his penis rose at an alarming rate. "I can just gobble you up." She tickled his navel with her tongue. He envisioned her going down on him and sucking him until he exploded inside her mouth. "I want you to take me from behind," Bethany said breathlessly. "I'm so hot."

Oh oh. It must be a hormonal change. He waited until she got into position with that delectable behind pointing in his direction. Her vaginal area was still wet with her juices. No spanking this time. He wouldn't do anything to shock her into losing their first child. He entered her gently.

"I'm not going to break, Al, and you entered the wrong hole."

Oh no she didn't. She couldn't mean that she wanted him to...

"Don't tell me you haven't thought about it?"

He moved inside of her and she backed that thing up against him. "Yes, on many occasions, but that takes a lot of concentration on my part, and quite frankly I don't think I can do it right now. He moved his hips back and forth feeling his jock slide in and out of her.

"Please make me come again."

How could he refuse? He met her grinds. Damn she was so hot, and she was so wet. Dripping to be exact. Was this how it was going to be for the remainder of the pregnancy? They were never ever going to leave the bedroom.

Bethany panted. "Deeper." She rocked on him. He let her have her way. Hell, she was doing pretty good without him. She stopped moving and slid him out of her and then pushed him on his back. "I want to ride." She mounted him, bouncing up and down on him like a wood nymph. Her breasts bounced enticingly in front of him. "Ooh, ooh, ooh," she repeated. "Just stay hard. Just stay hard."

"I'm trying to honey, but I'm afraid you're going to break it if you don't slow down."

"Don't be silly. Oh wow, that feels so good."

He had had enough. She was seriously scaring the shit out of him now. "Whoa, cowgirl." He rolled her off him. "My turn to lead." Maybe the baby would be okay. He raised her thighs and moved into her. "You want it deep?"

"Yes."

He plowed into her. "Come for me, my princess." He shoved his hips and sent his penis sailing into her. She responded by rewarding him with a warm flow of love juices that proved fatal. He went off like a bottle rocket. *Damn, too soon.* Bethany threw her arms around him. "I love you, Al."

Al sighed. Their baby would definitely have behavioral issues.

Yahi and Jamaal decided to drive to Mauritania to give Emir the good news instead of taking the horses. Besides they were still laying low. The newspaper had printed the retraction about the engagement, and Prince Yahi was reported to be ecstatic about the news. He left Bethany behind to await the autopsy report on the two mummies, hoping that she would finally get herself to a doctor. Hopefully she'd make it into the second trimester without a problem.

"What's wrong, Yahi?" Jamaal asked as they neared the compound.

"Baby problems. I'm sure I'm supposed to be making some type of preparations for his birth, like marrying his mother or something, but instead I'm fighting with her and raging hormones. She nearly castrated me last night."

Jamaal chuckled. "How?"

"Man, I couldn't do anything but lay there. She just took control like she was the man."

"Your chauvinistic ways are showing, Yahi. So she had her way with you. I read somewhere that pregnant women crave sex all the time."

"I'll never survive."

Jamaal drove up to the gate. The guards opened and waved them in. "Let's not mention that to Papa. My engagement will be enough for him to handle."

Yahi agreed. He hadn't confided in anyone except Jamaal and only because he was his best friend. But he was right. It was his time to shine. At the rate they were going he and Bethany would probably be married in the delivery room.

"Jamaal, Yahi," Jasmin shouted when they walked into the palace.

Jamaal grabbed his baby sister and hugged her tightly. He released her and she tackled Yahi. "Where is Bethany?"

"At work."

"Aw, I miss her. Papa said she's the best thing that happened to you in years."

"Papa is right this time."

"I can't believe I heard that?" Abdul said as he entered the foyer. "Jamaal, come give Papa a hug."

Jamaal hugged his father. "What brings you two demons here?"

"Jamaal has something to tell the family."

"Sounds important," Abdul said as they walked into the throne room.

"It is. Where is Mama?"

"Jasmin, go get Mama and Khalaf. They're in the kitchen."

Jasmin hurried off and returned with her mother and older brother. Nailah hugged Jamaal and Yahi.

"What's all the excitement about?" Khalaf asked. He was dressed in real clothes for once, and he was alert.

"Jamaal has some sort of announcement," Abdul replied.

"Papa, Mama, I have asked Kasia to marry me and she has accepted."

There was silence for a moment and then laughter as Abdul hugged him again. Jasmin and Nailah danced around. "A wedding?" Nailah clapped her hands. "I thought Yahi would beat you to the altar, but Kasia? We're going to finally get some grandchildren, Papa."

Khalaf grinned at his younger brother. "You finally roped her. Man, you're going to go broke trying to support her."

Yahi nodded. "That's the same thing I told him."

"Maybe your father will give us that little black credit card as a wedding present," Jamaal replied.

"No way. She's going to be your responsibility, Prince Hatem."

"Where's Bethany?' Khalaf asked.

"Working. The autopsies on those mummies should be back any day now."

"So, you've been to the tomb?"

Yahi nodded. "It's huge and has many chambers. There are many rooms filled with treasure and artifacts."

"Your father must be ecstatic," Abdul replied. "He has been searching since he was a boy."

"Yes, he is. We're taking him down to see it in a couple of days."

"Who's this Mark fellow we've been reading about in the newspaper?" Nailah asked.

"An old boyfriend," Jamaal answered for Yahi. "He is a swindler and wants Bethany for her money."

"She has money?"

Yahi nodded. "Her father was a famous American archeologist and her mother was a French fashion designer."

"Was?" Nailah asked.

"Yes, her mother died a couple of years ago, and her father was recently murdered."

Nailah gasped. "The poor girl. She is an orphan?"

"Not quite. She has an older brother but I don't think the two of them are close."

"You have to bring her back for a visit."

"I still haven't figured out a way to explain knowing you when she finds out that Jamaal is your son."

"That's because you weren't honest with her the last time you were here. She thinks that you are a criminal," Nailah reminded him. She hit him on the arm and then squeezed his chin affectionately. "Who could mistake that face for anything but an angel?"

"I'll tell her everything before she leaves."

"Leaves, where is she going?"

"Her job here is almost over. She will be returning back to the United States soon."

"No, Yahi. You have to stop her."

"Enough about me. Let us celebrate. Jamaal is about to lose his freedom."

Khalaf passed the pipe to Yahi, but he declined and passed it to Jamaal. "What's wrong?"

"Giving it up," Yahi replied. "There's still some stuff I can't remember from the last time."

Khalaf laughed. "You are such a wimp, Yahi."

Jamaal exhaled. "He sure is."

Yahi pouted. "I am not. I need all my energy for other things."

"Like what?" Khalaf asked as he accepted the pipe back from Jamaal and inhaled.

"Like Bethany," Jamaal answered, nearly choking on the smoke.

"Still living the double life?"

Yahi nodded. "But I plan to put an end to it soon. I don't think my jock can take it."

Khalaf looked at him oddly. "You mean she's doing both of you?"

"Yes."

"And you don't have a problem with this?"

"I didn't at first, but now I think I'm jealous of myself."

Khalaf inhaled. "That's stupid."

Jamaal continued to laugh. "I told him the same thing. But he's getting twice as much sex."

That caught Khalaf's attention. "Really?"

Yahi shrugged his shoulders. "The woman likes variety."

"So what's the problem?"

"She nearly broke my penis off last night. She was grinding into me until she had this super colossal orgasm that nearly knocked us off the bed."

Khalaf and Jamaal looked at each other. "I should have your problem," Khalaf admitted.

Jamaal agreed. "At least you're having sex. I have to wait until my wedding night."

"Why?" Yahi asked.

"She's a princess."

"Oh, yeah, I forgot about that old tradition. But you have my blessing if you want to knock the little man out of the boat before then."

"You should have seen the little belly-dancer Bethany when she was here."

"I heard," Jamal replied.

Khalaf laughed. "She had poor Yahi under a spell with those hips."

"You should see her in a bikini."

Khalaf sat up. "You've seen her in a bikini?"

"Sister has back, front, and everything else going on."

Yahi cleared his throat. "Excuse me. You're talking about the woman both me and Al-Shar loves."

Jamaal laughed and took the pipe from his older brother.

"I don't know what you're worried about. After all she is legally your wife," Khalaf replied.

Jamaal nearly choked again. "What?"

"Oh, didn't he tell you. Papa married them."

"What?"

"Tell him the whole story, Khalaf," Yahi replied.

"They were both high from the water pipe and Yahi was miserable because she was sexually torturing Al-Shar, so Papa and I woke them up partially and he married them."

"Ooh," Jamal said. "What did Bethany say when you told her."

"I haven't," Yahi confessed. "She thought I was a bandit and besides, we woke up naked with the sheets in a tangled mess like we had the best sex ever, and neither one of us remembered. The next thing I knew Mark was riding off into the sunset with her."

"Oh, what a wicked web we weave when we practice to deceive."

Yahi pushed Jamal over on a pillow. "You're stoned."

"Yes and your life is a mess."

Al-Shar kissed Bethany good-bye and drove off. He had been away for a week and just had to see her. And spend some time with her. She had calmed down. In fact, she was nearly mellow like how she was with Yahi. There was no doubt in his mind that she was indeed pregnant. Her clothes were starting to get too tight for her and he thought he would have to go shopping by Armana for her. His cell phone rang. He didn't recognize the number. "Hello."

"Hello. Al-Shar. This is Mark Kauffman. I think we need to meet."

"Where?" Al asked.

Mark gave him the directions. Al drove toward the address. He dialed Jamaal and filled him in on what was about to happen. He wondered what Mark was up to since they weren't supposed to meet again until he married Bethany. "Are you sure you're going to be okay until we get there?" Jamaal asked.

"Sure. I'm always prepared."

Mark was waiting for him on a long stretch of road outside of Luxor. He got out of the car and walked toward him. "What do you want, Kauffman. Are the two of you married yet?"

"No, she turned me down again."

"What are you talking about?"

"Bethany turned down my marriage proposal and gave me back that expensive diamond ring I gave her."

"I'm sorry to hear that. That means you won't need me to do her in."

"Yes." Mark pulled a gun and pointed it at him. Al just stood there. "I kept wondering why? Why won't she marry me? Was it because she was dating that prince? No. Was it because I was ugly? No. Then I asked myself why again?"

"Maybe because you left her for another woman before. She told me all about it."

"No, so I couldn't figure it out so I followed her tonight. I just had to find out what was going on in her life, and then I saw her with you."

"We're just friends."

Mark cocked the pistol. "No, you're not. You kidnapped her and now you're using her."

"You know I didn't kidnap her. And I didn't force her to stay with me for two weeks, nor do I control her in any kind of way."

"You've fucked her, haven't you?"

"I can't deny that. We have had intercourse. She's very good in the sack."

Mark frowned. "That's why I have to do what I have to do. I can't let you interfere with my plans." He raised the gun higher and before he could fire, Al raised his foot and kicked him aside the head. The gun flew from his hand and landed on the dark ground. Mark wobbled, but he didn't fall.

"Fight me like a man," Al told him. "We don't need weapons."

"You're scum. You think Bethany will stay with you? You're a dirty rotten murdering crook." He swung at him. Al ducked and punched him in the gut. Mark went down on one knee but rose.

"I might be all that, but Bethany loves me."

Mark swung again. This one landed against Al's jaw. The blow was solid, but Al did not flinch. "She does not."

He swung back. This one knocked Mark off his feet. He landed on his behind. "She does so. It's not your name she screams while we're making love. It's mine." He looked down for the gun, but it was out of his reach and real close to Mark.

Mark came up with the gun. "No, but she'll be crying at your funeral. I'll take care of you and then that arrogant prince." He fired. The bullet whizzed through the air, hitting Al in the shoulder.

Jamaal and the guards arrived just as he was losing consciousness. Mark climbed into his car and drove off. "The prince has been shot," one of the guards shouted. "He's bleeding everywhere."

He remembered hearing voices and being put into a car and then nothing else.

CHAPTER 20

"You are one lucky bastard," Jamaal said to him as he opened his eyes. Yahi tried to focus.

"How come I feel like someone has stuck a hot poker into my arm?"

"That's because Mark shot you."

"Oh, yeah, I remember."

"The authorities are looking for him."

"That's good."

"What happened?"

"We got into a fight over Bethany. I think he found out that she was secretly meeting me. He was upset because she refused to marry him."

"She's waiting in the lobby."

"What?" He reached for his face to feel for the mask.

"Your mother called her. We got the mask off you before we reached the hospital. Too much to explain to the doctors and nurses."

"How did you explain what I was doing out there on the road alone?"

"I told them it had to be a robbery. Someone must have been following you on your way home from a business meeting in Cairo."

"A good one. Now how am I going to explain matching injuries on both Yahi and Al-Shar to her?"

"You'll come up with something. Shall I send her in?"

Yahi nodded. "Let's get this over with."

Her eyes were bloodshot from crying and she looked as though she hadn't slept for days. But she was beautiful to him. "Your Highness. You're awake."

"Didn't I tell you to call me Yahi? We are far past the formal stage of our relationship."

She walked over to the bed with tears in her eyes. "I thought I lost you."

"Don't cry. You'll make yourself sick. It's just a flesh wound."

"It is not a flesh wound. The bullet went straight theough. Luckily whoever shot you had poor aim."

"It was Mark Kauffman."

Bethany gasped. "What?"

Yahi nodded. "I guess he has this grudge against me for loving you."

"What happened?"

"I really don't know. I was on my way home when this car bumped me from the rear. I got out checking the damage and he got out of the car and just shot me. He told me it was my fault that you did not want to marry him."

"That fool. I turned him down because he's a lying crook. I saw him pocket some of the jewels from that chest in the tomb."

Yahi smiled. "How do you get yourself surrounded by such unscrupulous men?"

Bethany wiped her eyes. "Just lucky I guess. Are you sure that you're all right?"

"I've had worse." He beckoned her closer. "I just need a kiss from you."

Bethany bent over the bed and kissed him softly on the lips. "Are you sure you're alright?"

"I'm just waiting on the doctor to give me the okay to leave this place. What about you? I heard you had the flu?"

"I'm almost over it."

"You need to see a doctor before you leave here just to make sure."

"Don't worry about me. I'm okay. You are the one who needs to get well."

"I told you that I was fine."

"You wouldn't admit it even if you were dying, would you?"

Yahi smiled. "No, now let's talk about you. What have you been up to?"

"I was making arrangements to go home until your mother called me."

Yahi tried to sit up. "No, don't go." He nearly pulled the IV out.

"Lay down, Yahi. You're going to rip your veins. I've already changed my plans. I'm not leaving. I've phoned my brother and told him I'd be staying a little while longer."

"What did he say?"

"He said, rock on baby sis, and I'll see you when I see you."

"Your brother sounds like quite a character."

"He is. He's probably romancing some sweet little starlet or something."

"Promise me that you won't leave until I get out of this hospital."

"I'm not going anywhere. In fact, your sister has asked me to be her maid of honor for her wedding to Jamaal."

"She what?"

"I was surprised too. Does Jamaal have a big family?"

"Yes. They're a laugh a minute. Especially his father and brother." He yawned.

"I'd better go. I'll send your family in."

"Okay."

She kissed him goodbye. "I'll check in on you later." He watched her leave. He was totally upset. In a span of a few minutes he had nearly missed out on the most important moment of his life. He'd get that bastard Kauffman if it was the last thing he did.

"How many flowers did you order, Yahi?" Kasia asked him as the floral arrangements began to arrive at the house for the wedding.

"Just a couple. It's not every day that my baby sister and my best friend gets married."

"Speaking of your best friend. You and Khalaf better not get him too high tonight at his bachelor party."

Yahi smirked. "Now would I do something like that?"

She sniffed the flowers. "Yes. Ooh, lilies. My favorite."

"I know."

She sat down. "Can I talk to you about something?"

He sat down next to her. "Sure." He rubbed his left arm. It was healing but he still had to wear a sling. "What do you want to talk about?"

"Sex."

"Huh?"

"You know. My wedding night."

"Shouldn't you be discussing this with mother?"

"Are you kidding? She blushes every time we talk about my period."

"Yeah, well, what do you want to know?"

"Everything."

"Let me rephrase this. How much do you already know?"

"I know how the mechanics are supposed to work, but I don't know how to do it so that Jamaal will find pleasure."

"All you have to do is get naked and smile."

"You're not helping."

"Listen. You will know. It's going to hurt at first, but I promise you that it'll get better. Don't concentrate on giving Jamaal all the pleasure. Think about yourself too. If it feels good, do it. You won't embarrass him if you want to do something freaky. He loves you."

Kasia jumped up and hugged him. "That's why I love you. You always know the right things to say." She turned him loose. "What time is Bethany arriving?"

"Around noon. I've sent a car for her and the others."

"Is she still trying to leave?"

"Yes, but I have to find a way to stop her."

"Why don't you ask her to marry you?"

"One wedding in this family is enough at the moment. Tomorrow is your big day."

She kissed him again and hurried off.

Yahi rubbed his sore arm. Bethany was now deep into her fourth month of pregnancy, and only a fool could not see it. Al-Shar had gone all out on her new wardrobe and had mysteriously disappeared for a month. He told Bethany he would be away for a while. A month had passed and he would soon be returning.

Jamaal was so stoned before the bachelor party was in full swing thanks to his wild father and equally deviant older brother. The wedding was a mere ten hours away and somehow, he had to let them celebrate, sober Jamaal up and get him to the palace on time. A jet was fueled and waiting to take them back to Cairo later.

Bethany was with his mother and had been recruited to go shopping with the women. That meant a lot of gossiping and a lot of spending money. The men, George, Andre, and Nicholas had flown down with him, and was having a whopping good time with Abdul, who was bombarding them with questions about the tomb and the mummies.

He had entertained the idea of getting Nicholas high on the pipe and asking him information about his feelings for Bethany, but even he wasn't that low. He had informed the guards to keep an eye out for Kaufmann and to shoot first and ask questions later if he put in an appearance. He wasn't ready to tell her about the contract on her head, but he planned to do it in the very near future.

The entertainment for the party had arrived. Jamaal woke up just in time to dance with some of the girls before passing out again. One of the young women danced over to him, smiling an invitation for him to sample her goods. He was flattered, but not interested. He would stay that way as long as he stayed sober and passed on the pipe.

"That woman has neutered you, Yahi," Khalaf replied after observing him for a while.

"She has not. I can do anything that I want to do."

"I beg to differ. You've passed on the pipe, and you've refused a very good invitation to bed a luscious young woman. The old Yahi would have taken her right here in front of us. What's wrong?"

"Nothing is wrong. I'm just taking a break. It's time I act a little responsible."

Khalaf laughed. "Why, has your father been on your case again?"

Yahi held up his injured arm. "The pain killers have me high enough."

"Does it still hurt?"

"A little. That bastard Kauffman tried to take my arm off."

"He caught you doing his fiancée. I would have shot you too."

"She is not his fiancée, and the other archeologists don't know about Al-Shar, so I'd prefer it stays that way."

"Perfectly understandable. You do intend to seek revenge."

"Oh, yeah, even though it was a lucky shot."

"I was meaning to ask you about that. How did he manage to hit you? You have several black belts in Karate and all that other martial arts stuff. Your father trained us to be killers."

"It was dark, and I had just kicked the gun from his hand. But apparently not far enough away. I won't make that mistake again."

"I can't believe that he actually contracted you to kill her. What was he thinking?"

"That she hated me for kidnapping her, and that I was greedy enough to do it for a price."

Bethany fidgeted as the seamstress put the finishing touches on her gown. "I think I made a mistake with your measurements a couple of weeks ago," the woman replied. "I have to take the seams out around the bust and waist."

Bethany bit her bottom lip thankful that no one else was around except them. If the seamstress suspected what she suspected, the media would blast the announcement before she confirmed it with a doctor. She had always prided herself in being a perfect size ten, but now her bra cups were overflowing. Nearly four months had passed since her last period and even she couldn't lie to herself anymore. She had snuck off to the hospital earlier and took a test and was waiting for them to call with the results.

"It won't take me but a few minutes to make the adjustments."

"Thank you," Bethany told her as she got back into her clothes. The faster the alterations were done the faster she could leave.

Less than an hour later she had the gown in the garment bag and headed to another store to pick up her shoes. Her feet, thankfully had not betrayed her. The last thing she wanted was to try to dance in tight shoes. Kasia and her mother were in the beauty salon when she arrived.

"How was the fitting?" Naadirah asked as she cleared a spot for her on a chair.

"Over at last. I gave the gown and my shoes to the chauffer, and he's guarding them with his life."

Naadirah nodded. "Everything has to be perfect. Yahi will kill us if it doesn't go exactly as planned."

Bethany smiled. "You would think that it his own wedding that he's planning."

Naadirah sighed. "I pray for that day to come. That Yahi is such a wild one. I'm glad that he's met you. He has calmed down some."

"I'm glad I met him too. He's the first real honest man I've met in a long time."

"And he's a pretty good lover too, huh?"

Bethany blushed.

"Aw, come on. I'm his mother. I know these things. His father is excellent in bed. Even at his age."

"Mother?' Kasia said quite shocked. "Really." "You've never been so open before about such things."

"Really. You better hope that Jamaal has learned a thing or two from your father and brother about pleasing a woman. He is such a shy young man. He's too fine to be a dud in bed. I've never spoke like this before in front of you is because you were my baby girl. You're a grown woman now and it's time you realize that men and woman were created to make love and have fun with each other. "

Kasia buried her head back under the dryer.

"I don't think she is going to have a problem tonight. I used to change Jamaal's diapers and let me tell you he was huge even back then."

The shampoo girl came over just in time to rescue her. Bethany followed her over to the sink. "Is there anything special you want done?"

"I think I need some of this hair cut off. The heat is making it grow at an alarming rate, and maybe a new color. Blonde hair and an off-white gown do not go. It will look washed out in the wedding pictures."

"You could wear a wig," Kasia suggested. "Then you won't have to mess up your hair."

The shampoo girl nodded. "We sell those. I have just the color. It's a chocolate brown with red highlights. It will not only bring out that dress, but those eyes and that tan."

"I hoped you stopped off at the lingerie shop," Kasia said once she saw Bethany's new hair color.

"Why?" Bethany asked.

"Because Yahi is going to go nuts when he sees you. He's got this thing for brunettes."

Bethany looked at herself in the mirror. So did Al-Shar. "Do you really think he'll like it?"

Kasia hugged her. "No, he's going to love it."

"Stop fidgeting, Jamaal," Yahi warned as he helped him into his ceremonial robes.

"I'm not fidgeting. This stuff is itchy."

"You'd be used to it by now if you hung out with your father more and did family stuff. All princes are supposed to dress like this every now and then."

"The man is not exactly easy to handle in long spurts of time."

Yahi laughed. "Don't I know it? I still owe him one for what he and Khalaf did to me."

"Don't' look at it as a trick. At least everything is legitimate if you know what I mean?"

"Yes, it is legal. My mother will be thankful for that when she finds out. She already thinks I'm going to hell anyway."

"Have you seen her yet?"

"No, I want my first glance at her to be when she walks down that aisle. At the rate things are going that might be the only chance I get to see her do it."

"Whose turn is it tonight?"

"Mine. Al-Shar is supposed to be back next week. I think."

"Dumb ass."

"Now, is that anyway to talk on your wedding day?"

"No, but it helps my nerves to see you suffer. Damn, my head still hurts."

"It's one of Malik's concoctions. It's guaranteed to knock you flat on your ass."

"It's hard to believe that Khalaf will be Emir one day. Hell, it's even harder to believe that Malik is a caliph. Khalaf is bad enough but the two of them together can destroy the world with their deviances."

Yahi nodded. "He might do a three-hundred and sixty degree turn and surprise you."

Jamaal laughed. "I don't think so. He has been around Papa too long."

Emir Abdul popped his head into the room. "It's almost show time." He entered. "I think you and I need to have a little man to man talk before you walk down the aisle."

"I already know about sex, Papa."

"Not about sex. It's about how to please a woman."

"I'm out of here," Yahi said.

"Coward," Jamaal called out behind him.

CHAPTER 21

Tears stung Yahi's eyes as Bethany made her way up the aisle to him. She wore a traditional off-white bridesmaid's gown that showed off her pretty shoulders, her deep tan, and those ever growing ta-tas. The bun in the oven was nicely disguised. It was hidden behind the folds of layer after layer of cloth and silk, and she wore a wig that he found quite sexy.

He walked up and escorted her rest of the way down the aisle, imagining that it was their wedding day. They parted company when they reached the end. All eyes turned to the door as Kasia appeared on the arm of their father. The brat, he had to admit, made a beautiful bride, and poor Jamaal trembled at his side. He looked like he was going to break into tears as he watched her approach.

Yahi would have liked to be a fly on the wall of their honeymoon suite to see if Abdul had taught him something new. But he planned to be quite busy later with a certain brown-haired, blue-eyed temptress whom he hadn't bedded since he had gotten wounded. He looked over at her halfway through the ceremony. Bethany looked green. *I hope she doesn't blow*, he mused. Kasia would never forgive her. Moments after the happy couple was pronounced man and wife, Yahi watched her sneak out of the ballroom and rush up to her room.

"Where's Bethany?" Jamaal asked him when he got a free moment away from his bride, well-wishers and the photographers.

"Up in her room with her head buried in the toilet."

"You think she knows?"

"I'm fairly certain of it."

Jamaal sighed. "Those ta-tas are amazing. They're like two big balloons."

"Down boy, you're married now."

"I can't wait until Kasia gets pregnant. I'm going to bury my head in her bosoms and never come out."

Yahi chuckled. "Yeah, I hope you get the chance to hold her hair back while she's throwing up real soon."

Bethany reappeared about an hour later talking to someone on her cell phone. She hung up before she approached. She had changed into yet another outfit that hid her ripening girth. The baby was well hidden under fabric and padding, but those breasts could not be contained. Color had returned to her cheeks, and men hovered around her like dogs in heat. It took him a while to rescue her so the two of them could be alone. He took her out to the back gardens where she could sit and rest.

"You look beautiful in that dress," Yahi told her as he sat next to her. "And I love your hair. It's really becoming."

"Really?"

He nodded.

"It's a wig. I wanted to try something new." She sighed. "It was a beautiful ceremony and Kasia made a lovely bride."

"Yes, and yes." He touched her cheek. It was damp. Had she been crying? "You looked as pretty as a bride too as you came down the aisle."

Bethany blushed. "Nonsense. I was just lucky that Kasia chose a lovely gown for me. Usually bride maids suffer a horrible fashion fate."

"Have you ever thought about getting married?"

"Of course. What girl hasn't? I used to dream of walking down the aisle in this white dress that had so much lace that I looked like a princess. It was the old fash-ioned kind with lots of tiny buttons down the back that would make my husband all upset just trying to unbutton them fast enough to get me into bed. And…"

"And what?"

"And my father would give me away."

"You miss him, don't you?"

She nodded. "I wasn't even there to say good-bye and now he's never going to…"

"Going to what?"

"Never mind."

"Have you heard from your brother yet?"

"Yes, the police haven't discovered anything except that they know that someone definitely was with my father the night that he died. They found two drink glasses. They're dusting them for prints." She sighed again. "I'm just glad he went quickly and didn't suffer."

"Would you like to go back to the ballroom and dance?"

"Would it be okay if we stay out here a little longer? The night is so beautiful."

"Yes."

"How is your arm? Is it still bothering you?"

"It's better."

"I can't believe that Mark tried to kill you."

"He is jealous."

"But you're the sweetest man I know."

He touched her cheek again. It was on the tip of his tongue to tell her the truth, but he could tell that she was upset about her father, and confused by the phone call she had received earlier.

"Don't pretend you don't know me," Khalaf said to Bethany when he finally got her alone later.

"Imagine how surprised I was to learn that Jamaal is actually your brother."

"It's a small world. Imagine my surprise to find out that you're dating the prince." The last time I checked you were into bandits." He took her arm. "Come dance with me."

Bethany allowed Khalaf to lead her to the dance floor. The music was slow and he held her close. "Did you tell Prince Yahi about Al-Shar?"

"No."

"I assume that they know each other, don't they?"

"I don't think so. Al-Shar and I grew up together in Mauritania. Our fathers are friends. He and Yahi don't travel in the same social circles." He laughed. "Yet they have the same tastes in women."

"I am not Al-Shar's woman."

"Bethany, dear. I was there when you danced for him, and I was there the next morning when you came down with bee-stung lips bruised by Al-Shar's kisses. And, I was there when you climaxed and screamed out his name."

Bethany pinched him. *Now what am I going to do?*

"Ouch. Don't worry. Your secret is safe with me."

"There is no secret. Yahi and I are just friends."

"He hasn't taken his eyes off you since you came down the aisle. And he's watching me right now ready to kick my ass if I step out of line."

"You exaggerate."

"No, I don't. What do you think he would do if I kissed you right now?"

"I don't know. But if I were you I would be less worried about Yahi and more concerned about what Al-Shar would do to you."

Khalaf laughed. "I thought you said you weren't his woman."

"Why are you torturing me, Khalaf? I thought we were friends."

"Maybe I'm jealous. Look at you. You're beautiful, and for some reason there is a glow about you."

"You are a gorgeous prince. You can have any woman that you chose. Why would you want me?"

"Because you have brought two of the most powerful men of Egypt to their knees." He twirled her around. "So the sex must be mind-blowing." The music ended and he walked her back to Yahi. "It has been a pleasure, Ms. Dailet." He turned to Yahi. "You must bring her to the palace for a visit." He bowed and walked away.

"Prince Khalaf appears to be overwhelmed by your beauty."

"Prince Khalaf has issues that only he can sort out. He's cute in a vulgar sort of way."

Yahi laughed. "Believe it or not, he would take that as a compliment." He led her back to the dance floor. "Now it's my time." He folded her into his arms and molded his body with hers. He felt something flutter against his stomach. It was faint but definitely a flutter. "Why are you tensing? Are you okay?"

"I'm a little tired. It's been a long day."

"I'm sure the happy couple won't mind if you slipped off and went to bed a little early."

"Would you be tucking me in?"

"Oh yes, and watching over you like a hawk until Khalaf leaves tomorrow."

Yahi snuck back down the stairs later once Bethany had dozed off. The happy couple had left for their honeymoon and the party was winding down. Khalaf was in the garden waiting for him.

"She's pregnant," Khalaf announced.

"Who?" Yahi asked.

"Bethany."

"How do you know that?"

"It's kind of hard to miss when you're dancing cheek to cheek with her."

"That was because you were practically trying to screw her through her clothes."

"Just having a little innocent fun. You know me. Now back to Bethany. You're the father, I suppose?"

"Me or Al-Shar."

Khalaf shook his head. "Don't play with me, Yahi. When are the two of you going to make the announcement? She holds the future king of Egypt in her womb."

"As soon as she tells me or him."

"What do you mean? She hasn't told you yet. How do you know?"

"I've known for quite some time. I know that body of hers. I watched it change. Did you see those breasts?"

"They're hard to miss. They are really out there. Who else knows?"

"Jamaal, but I have sworn him to secrecy."

"It isn't going to be a secret long. What is she two months?"

189

"Four."

Khalaf stared at him. "When do you think she's going to tell you, when she's on the delivery table?"

Yahi shrugged his shoulders. "She won't be able to hide it much longer. I got the feeling that she's about to jump ship and run back to the United States."

"Why would she do something like that?"

"She's depressed about her father's death and she's pregnant by one of two men that she's slept with. All of that is eating at her conscious."

"Put her out of her misery. Tell her the truth."

"She is going to hate me."

"She is your wife."

"She doesn't know that either."

"That's your fault. You should have told her the moment I told you."

"This is true. And I guess I have to thank you and Papa for doing it before our child was conceived."

"You're welcome. Can I be the god-father?"

"I don't know. The child will have issues enough with just me being its father."

"It could be worse, I could be the father."

"Are you going to try to fuck her once she delivers?"

"I don't know. I might."

Yahi hit him on the arm. "You're a wonderful friend, but you're a lousy bastard, Prince Hatem."

"It takes one to know one, Prince Amasis."

"Whoopee," Hathor shouted after he hung up the phone. "The results are in. It's a king." He danced around the room as the others came through the door. "It is confirmed. The mummy in the first sarcophagus was Pharaoh Amasis. The DNA sample Prince Yahi gave to us to use matched perfectly. It was as close as if they were father and son."

"What about the other one?" George asked.

"It's a queen. His queen to be exact. And get this. She was a brunette. There was still hair attached to the mummy."

George and Andre joined in the dance while Nicholas went off to fix some drinks for them to toast with.

"Where's Bethany?" Andre asked.

"She went out early this morning," George answered. "She had a doctor's appointment."

"It's about time. If she gets any bigger I'm afraid that I will have to deliver the little prince myself."

George scratched his head. "You know too. I thought I was the only one that figured it out."

Hathor laughed. "Nope. We all know. Those breasts are huge."

Nicholas entered the room. "I wonder who the father is." He handed each of them a drink."

"What do you mean?" Andre asked. "It's Prince Amasis."

"Are you sure? From what I can tell she's about four or five months pregnant, and we've been here just that long. And in that time, she's had several men sniffing around her including me," Nicholas replied.

"Are you saying that you could be the father?" George asked.

"No, I never got the chance to rock her world."

"Mark Kauffman?"

Nicholas nodded. "It's a possibility. After all, she was very much in love with him but I don't think it's his."

"Then whose?" Andre asked.

"She was gone for two weeks. Two weeks when we didn't know where she was. Two weeks that she never quite explained."

George gulped. "Al-Shar."

Nicholas nodded. "Didn't you notice how different she acted when she returned? He probably raped her."

George shook his head. "I don't think so. He's in love with her."

Andre eyed George curiously. "What are you keeping from us?"

"I've met him. He and I have been working together on a little project."

"Why?" Nicholas asked. "He's a wanted criminal."

"He's trying to protect Bethany. I guess I might as well come out and tell you everything, but you guys have to promise me that you won't mention it to a soul."

The other men promised.

"Mark Kauffman killed Ernest Dailet and he tried to get Bethany to marry him."

Nicholas nearly choked on his drink. "What?"

"That's not all. He tried to hire Al-Shar to kill Bethany after the marriage so he could collect the insurance money and her inheritance. And when she turned him down he shot Prince Amasis because he thought the Prince was the reason she turned him down. Al-Shar pretended to go along with him, and set a trap to catch him."

The door behind them shut. Everyone turned around. Bethany stood there in shock. Something fell from her hand and hit the floor.

"How much did you hear?" George asked.

"Everything." She ran to her room crying.

"I guess I better go to her," George said. "I think she's going to need a shoulder to cry on."

Nicholas stopped him. "She needs time to be alone." He stopped and picked up the bag that Bethany dropped. It was from the pharmacist. He pulled the prescription out. "Prenatal vitamins."

The tears kept coming and coming until Bethany couldn't cry anymore. "It's your own fault for being a pop-tart," she said aloud. "What were you thinking doing the mattress mambo with two men?" It was clearer now. It was all her fault that Yahi got shot. He was innocent in all of this. The baby moved inside of her. So now what was she going to do? "The only thing I can do. I'm going home until the baby is born. If he or she is blond it's Yahi. If he has dark hair it's Al-Shar's." She shook her head. "That's not right. Yahi's father and sister have dark hair, and who knows, maybe Al-Shar was a blond under the hood and mask. The only way to find the true identity of the father was to have a paternity test performed. Well she couldn't wait four more months because her belly button had pushed out and there was just no way to explain that.

Her telephone rang. It was Yahi.

"I just heard the wonderful news about the mummy. It has been confirmed that it is King Amasis, and the other one is his wife."

"I'm glad for you. I know it means a lot to you and your family."

"I'm just calling to tell you that I have to go out of town for a week."

"Where?"

"To the Netherlands. It's a political function. I can't get out of it."

"Have fun," she replied. "We'll do lunch when you return."

"We'll do more than lunch, Ms. Dailet," he whispered.

Bethany giggled. "I'll see you when you get back." She hung up the phone. Good, she would be gone by the time he returned. Now all she had to do was make her arrangements, do a little shopping and she still had another doctor's appointment. She looked down at her watch. It was getting late.

"Are you sure you're going to be okay all by yourself tonight?" George asked as he fixed his tie. "I hate to leave you with that lunatic still running around."

"Mark is probably long gone by now. He's a wanted man in two countries."

"There are plenty of places to hide over here."

Bethany shook her head. "His skin is too pale to blend in. Anyway, I have my cell phone. I'll call the police the moment I hear a sound."

"Let's hope that nothing will happen. I feel bad that you're going to miss the presentation. If it wasn't for you none of this would be happening." The archeologists were being honored in Sais for the work they had done and the discovery of the former royals. They would be gone a couple of days—just long enough for her to leave before they got back. "I left my gun in my nightstand. Don't be afraid to use it."

"No problem. If he comes here I'll take him out of this world."

"I believe you would, honey, but remember you have another life depending on you now."

"I know. I'll be careful."

It was strange now that it wasn't a secret anymore. They were all treating her like fragile glass and touching her stomach…even Hathor. Her flight was scheduled to leave at six in the morning. She would eat, get a good night's sleep and take a taxi to the airport. It was around nine when she finally wore herself out enough to go to sleep. A sound woke her up around midnight.

Bethany slowly opened her eyes. A masked man stood over her bed looking down on her.

"Good evening sweet, Bethany."

She sat up. "Al-Shar. You nearly scared the life out of me. What are you doing here?"

"Is that any way to welcome me after I've been gone for nearly a month?"

"Where have you been?"

"I went to the United States."

"Why?"

"It was business."

"Okay, if you say so."

He spotted the suitcases. "Are you going somewhere?"

She nodded, finding it hard to keep her eyes off him. He wore a black do-rag, a mask, a black long sleeved shirt, and tight low riding pants. He was even wearing some unusual gold jewelry. Dark brown eyes bore down on her. She nodded. "Yes."

"Where?"

"Away."

"That's not smart."

"I have to leave here. There's a contract on my head."

Al stopped. "You know?"

She nodded again. "Mark tried to kill Prince Amasis."

"The royal whelp?"

"Yes, and it's my fault because I turned down his marriage proposal."

"So why did he shoot Amasis?"

"Because Mark thinks that the two of us are lovers."

"Are you?"

She just stared at him. He sat down on the bed and stroked her arm. "Someone might come in."

"Don't try it. I know that you are alone. I watched the others leave. They are on their way to Sais."

"How do you find these things out?"

"It's my job."

"What job is that?"

"I'm a protector of the innocent." He bent over and kissed her arm.

Bethany shuddered. *This was not going to be easy. Maybe he won't notice the difference if we do it in the dark.*

"You haven't answered me." He moved up her arm with his kisses.

"That's because you might not like the answer."

He stopped and stared at her with those dark brown eyes. He rose. "So it is true? You have slept with the prince?" He turned his back on her.

"Yes."

He spun around. "When? Why?"

"I don't know. It just happened. He's really very sweet."

"Sweet? Men are not sweet. I think I shall kill him."

Bethany sat up. "No, please don't."

Al turned around. "Look at you, pleading for his life. Is he that good in bed?"

Bethany backed up to the pillow afraid to answer. "He's gentle."

"But you don't like it gentle. You like it when I push it in deep."

"Stop, Al-Shar. This is hard enough."

"You don't know hard." He walked back over to the bed and snatched her hand up. He put it against his penis. "Feel this. This is hard. It wants to impale you."

She snatched her hand away. "I can't. Not now."

He pulled her into his arms. "You think that I care that you let some little royal punk screw you?" He pushed her back down on the bed and began to remove his clothes. He tore off his shirt, unbuttoned his pants, and removed his briefs.

His body was magnificent. He swaggered back over to the bed. "You're mine." He pulled the covers from the bed. Bethany tried to hide behind the pillows.

"I will scream."

"That's exactly what I had in mind." He grabbed her legs and tugged her to him. She kicked at him and he just laughed. He reached up and yanked the flimsy gown from her body, flipped her over onto her knees. She was naked and vulnerable. "I'm about to give you something your prince never will." He spat on his finger and shoved it up her rectum. Bethany yelped and tried to get away from him. He held her with his other arm. She struggled, causing his injured arm to hurt. "Keep still you little filly and let a real man show you how it's done." He removed the finger, wet another, and shoved them both in.

"Ow," Bethany moaned. "That hurts."

"Not as much as what's coming behind them." He removed his fingers, pulled a condom out of the folds of his do-rag, and put it on. Then he spread her cheeks and pushed the head of his penis near her anus.

"Don't do this," she begged.

He popped her on the butt. "Why not? You wanted me to before." He shoved his hips and the head entered.

Bethany gasped with pleasure.

"See, I knew you'd like it."

I must be sick. Her anger quickly turned as she rocked back on his penis. It slid into her, giving her the strangest feeling. He was so big, and it felt like he could rip her apart. Al-Shar was still angry...disgusted with her for succumbing to Yahi. He fondled her breast, pinching her nipples until they budded and grew hard. With the other hand, he dipped into her vagina. Tantalizing sensations ripped through her as she strained against him. He was brutally powerful as he continued to pound away in her behind. *The baby*, she thought. *I have to stop him.* "Al," she said breathlessly. "You're hurting me."

He stopped and carefully withdrew. Bethany lowered her behind and turned over on her back. She scrambled up to the pillows. Al stepped off the bed, removed the condom and headed into the bathroom. She heard the shower turn on, and a few minutes later he came out. She was still naked and hiding beneath the covers.

"Why didn't you run while I washed the evil from me?"

"I was afraid to."

He turned on the light and walked over to her. His erection was gone. "I am sorry. I shouldn't have abused you that way. Anal sex should be a beautiful thing shared between lovers." The covers slipped from her grasp as he sat down on the bed. Her breasts were still in an aroused state.

"There's something I need to tell you," Bethany said as she saw his eyes go down to her exposed breasts.

He reached out and touched one of them. "They are swollen and much fuller than I remember."

"That's what I need to tell you."

He moved in closer and nuzzled against them. He took one of the nipples between his lips and sucked. The baby moved beneath the covers behind which she hid. Al slurped like he was eating a lollipop. He pawed the other one with his free hand. Her head went back and her eyes closed as the sensations rolled through her.

"What do you have to tell me, Bethany?" He worked his face into them. "They're like pillows." He buried his face between her breasts. "I am so turned on. I have to be inside you." He kissed the breast. "I'm sorry for acting like such an ass earlier. I was so jealous." He pushed her down on the pillow. "I love you." He lowered his head and kissed her neck, working his way down her breast again. Bethany continued to clutch the cover around her bottom half. "What do you want to tell me, my sweet?" He licked below the breast, down her belly.

Bethany let the sheet go and revealed her secret.

Al-Shar paused, looking down on her very prominent navel. He roared proudly, spread her legs, and impaled her.

CHAPTER 22

*B*ethany crept out of the bed, trying to find the way around the room in the darkness. She made it to the bathroom to relieve her aching bladder. The nausea had subsided and had been replaced by frequent bouts of urination.

She turned on the shower and stepped beneath the spray. She ached all over, including her behind that Al-Shar kissed and apologized for forcefully sodomizing her. She smiled, knowing that she had loved every moment of it. The smile faded. What was she thinking? She didn't have time for this. Her plane was leaving in a couple of hours and she still had to reserve a taxi.

Bethany left the bathroom light on so she could see, and so she would not disturb him while he slept. He was flat on his back, with nothing on except his mask and rings. The idea of snatching the mask off was tempting, but she decided that she didn't want to anger him again. Something was missing. *Where the hell are my suitcases?*

She frowned. He probably moved them while she slept. Well, if he thought that was going to stop her he didn't know her very well. She dressed and then searched through the closet for the luggage. She didn't find it. She tip-toed over to the bed to find her watch on the night stand. That's when she noticed something on the pillow case. It was blood. One of them was bleeding. She hurried back into the bathroom to check herself. Nope, it wasn't her. Maybe she had raked his back too deep with her nails. Yes, that could be it. Then she saw the bandage. It was flesh-colored, and almost invisible to the eyes.

Al-Shar was injured, and the cut had reopened. She wondered how it had happened. Upon closer examination, she noticed a blue line, extending from beneath the bandage and heading up his arm. Prince Amasis had a similar mark. She gasped. Al had been shot just like him. She reached out to touch it. Al grabbed her hand.

"What do you think you're doing?"

"You're injured."

Al tried to cover the wound. "It's nothing."

She climbed onto the bed. "You've been shot."

"It's just a flesh wound."

Now where had she heard that before? She climbed off the bed and went to get her first aid kit. "How did it happen?" she asked as she patched him back up.

"Someone ambushed me. I don't know who. All I remember was waking up in a hospital."

"I think it was Mark Kauffman. Yahi has a similar wound."

Al stared at her. "Yahi? You say his name so tenderly."

She backed away. He was still angry.

"Look at you. You are carrying my seed deep inside of you, and still you think of him."

"You're wrong. I'm concerned about what happened to both of you. Mark is crazy and he won't stop until he kills someone."

"He already has. Mark killed your father."

"No," Bethany gasped. "So it is true?"

"Yes, I found out while I was in the United States. Your brother said one of the maids remembered hearing the two of them talking. And then the detectives discovered the two glasses they used. The prints matched your father's and Marks."

"Oh, my god."

"That's why you can't go back home. I can't protect you there. My assets and contacts are here."

Her bottom lip quivered and tears rushed from her eyes. He pulled her into his arms. "There, there. It's going to be all right. I'm going to find Kauffman and turn him over to the authorities long before the baby is born."

Bethany cried harder. How was she going to explain this baby to Yahi?

Two days later, her phone rang. It was Yahi. "I came back early," he told her. "And I need to see you. I have reserved a room at a nearby hotel so bring enough things for an over-nighter."

It was on the tip of her tongue to say no, but she had no other choice, because she really couldn't keep her secret any longer. There was just no way to hide that belly. She had to get it all out in the open before the unveiling of the artifacts to the public that would be happening in a couple of days. All eyes would be on her and the royal family. The fellows had returned and were off at the museum helping to catalog the finds. Normally that would be her job, but she was hiding. She told them that she was going to meet Yahi. She couldn't hide their relationship anymore since they all assumed it was his baby. There was a fifty-fifty chance that it was.

A box with a beautiful dress, lingerie and shoes arrived from Yahi. It came from Armana's store. Bethany blushed. The lingerie was positively shocking. She hoped Armana would not mention that little fact to Nicholas, who was barely speaking to her. He just walked around looking hurt. Well, she didn't have time to mend his fractured feelings. She had to go break the heart of the crowned prince of Egypt.

She stopped at the reservation desk at the hotel and gave her name. The person behind the desk handed her a pass key to the penthouse. She was a little apprehensive at first, expecting Mark to be there instead of Yahi. She opened the door and was nearly blind-sided by the flowers. There was food on the table, soft romantic music playing on the stereo, sparkling cider in the ice bucket and a very sexy Yahi sprawled out on the bed sleeping in black lounging pajamas. His hair was still damp from washing, and he smelled fresh and clean like soap and cologne. He opened his eyes when he felt her in the room.

"Hello beautiful."

She smiled at him. "Did I disturb you?"

"No, I was just taking a power nap." He yawned, stretched and then crawled out of the bed. "Do you like the dress?"

"Yes, it's lovely. Thank you."

"And the lingerie?"

"Hmm, yes, thanks. Hopefully Armana is discrete. They're crotchless."

"I have always fantasized of making love to a woman in crotchless panties." He kissed her and led her toward the other room. "Would you like to eat now or later?"

"Later. I feel like dancing."

She felt so good in his arms. "I've wanted to hold you for a long time. Since way before the wedding." He hadn't touched her that night. She was still too ill with morning sickness.

"How did your meeting go with the Netherlands?"

"We are allies. So it's always a good thing when we meet to talk shop."

"Have you heard from Kasia and Jamaal?"

He nodded. "Yes. They have returned from their honeymoon. They send their love."

He danced her over to the cider. "None for me."

"It's non-alcoholic." He danced her and the cider into the bedroom.

"You're surprisingly light on your feet, Prince Amasis."

He kissed her. "I've missed you ever so much, Ms. Dailet. It has been a long time since we've had a meeting of our two countries."

Bethany giggled. It was like music to his ears. "Is that what it's called now?"

He poured the cider and handed her a glass. It was good and cold. "Yes. We are about to combine forces. My flag is already at half-mast." He followed her eyes down.

"Ooh, I think it is."

He took the glass away from her, spun her around, and slid the zipper of dress down. She stepped out of the dress with her back to him and then spun around. Yahi pointed to her stomach. "What is that pointing at me?"

"My navel."

"I don't remember you having an outie."

"Usually I don't."

"Is there something you wish to tell me, Ms. Dailet?"

"Yes. Cider makes me fat."

Yahi dropped down to his knees at her feet. "You're pregnant."

"Yes, almost five months."

He counted on his fingers. "Oh my. That would mean that I might possibly be the father."

She stepped away from him. "Probably." She turned displaying an ass to die for encased in crotchless red panties and very high stiletto heels.

"That would explain those sudden bouts of sickness and you nearly passing out in the tomb."

She removed the bra. Those amazing breasts bobbed just above her stomach. His penis rose to attention. She never looked sexier. "Well aren't you going to say anything?"

Yahi rose, swept her up into his arms and tenderly put her on the bed. "Before I cover your private parts in cherry flavored lube, will you do me the honor of becoming my wife?"

Bethany cracked a smile. "I think that has to be the worse marriage proposal ever."

Yahi smiled. "Yes, you're right. I'm sorry. I have strawberry flavored too."

Bethany edged up the headboard as Yahi did sinfully wonderful things to her with his mouth. He had her propped up on a pillow with one under her butt and the other over her stomach to protect the baby. His tongue played deeply inside of her, swirling around like he was trying to lick her insides out. There was a lot of slurping and sucking noises, and her labia and clitoris were both wet and sticky from saliva and lube. She grabbed his hair as her body stretched. He nibbled around the sensitive areas.

"Yahi," she screamed. "I think I'm about to set sail." He buried tongue deeper. "Oh, ah, yes, yes."

"Wow," Yahi said as he came up for air. "That was a gusher." He put his head back down and licked her clean. "I could lie down there and eat you all night," he said as he raised his head again.

Bethany sat up. "You're sticky."

"Yeah, and we're about to buy the hotel some new sheets because we're going to get even stickier." He kissed her on the stomach. "You will have to cover my son's eyes, while I disrobe."

Bethany placed her hands on the pillow and watched him slide the briefs down his slim hips. That beautiful bare penis rose. She smirked. It was amazing, like Al-Shar's...a perfect head and big balls. No wonder she couldn't decide between the two of them. Everything about them was almost identical. She mused. Would it be a hoot if they were actually twin brothers? *Oh my.* Is that possible? Khalaf said they didn't know each other, but he could have lied. Maybe he was King Wahid's outside child. Shit, what if it was true? It would explain how Al-Shar could afford that car and those houses.

Yahi walked over to the side of the bed and lubed himself. "I hope you're not allergic to strawberries."

She turned to the side and opened her mouth. "Let me taste it first."

"Ooh, you're in a good mood. Tonsil hockey. I'm into that." He pushed his penis past her lips and down her throat. He held her head while he worked his hips. The head of the penis touched her tonsils making her gag. Yahi let her up for air. "Strawberries, nuts and a banana. All that is missing is the ice cream."

Yahi smiled. "Are you craving ice cream? I can handle that if you like. Give me a few minutes."

She grinned as he went down her throat again. Her vagina reacted by moving and trying to suck in the sheets. She moved her mouth around, sucking on him, trying to get the semen to wake up. Yahi's head went back and his hips undulated as she tried to milk him. After a while she realized that he was toying with her. "You're not even close, are you?"

He pulled out before she could clamp down on him with her teeth. "No," He bent down and kissed her on the lips. "I don't think I'm multi-orgasmic. It's a one shot deal and I'm saving the best for last."

She wondered what he meant by that. Her flipped her over on her stomach, raised her buttocks and squirted lube between her butt cheeks. "What are you doing your highness?"

"I'm looking for a condom."

He fumbled around in the drawer next to the bed. "Is this your private penthouse?"

"Yes, why?"

"Do you always keep condoms in the night stand?"

"Yes, why?"

"How many women have you entertained up here?"

"Does it matter? And stop asking questions. You're breaking my concentration."

"It matters to me."

"Let's just say I used to entertain before I met you." He removed the condom from the foil, stretched it, and slid it on.

"You do realize that I'm pregnant."

"Um hum. Two different holes. The baby will be perfectly safe while his parents get freaky."

"You're pretty sure it's a boy?"

"Yes. I am a prince of Egypt. My male sperm is dominant. Now just relax."

"Ah!" Bethany moaned as he entered her rectum. Her body opened and accepted him. It didn't hurt quite as much as it had when Al-Shar did it. Lube was definitely the answer.

Yahi straddled her butt. His technique was different than Al's. He could stroke better from this position. "You have the sexiest ass in the world." He moaned as he moved in and out of her, then he smacked her on the butt cheek.

"Ouch." He rubbed it like Al-Shar did. Like that was supposed to take away the pain.

"You've been very naughty, Ms. Dailet."

Bethany's eyes widened. "Yes, very naughty. Punish me, Yahi."

He pulled out slowly and then sank back in. "Ah," he moaned. "I'm so close." He pulled out again slowly. He shivered above her. "Uh," he groaned as he went back in. "Darn." He popped her on the cheek again. "Do you like what I'm doing to you?"

"Yes, my prince. My pussy is soaking wet."

He popped her again. "Pussy? Where did you learn such a word?"

"I read it on the walls in the ladies restroom."

He nearly sat down on top of her behind. This movement forced him in deeper. "I seem to have you at an advantage. I can split you in two from this position."

"You'll kill your son."

He withdrew a little and sank back in. Her body shuddered. How could that be? He was not in her vagina. He bounced around a little. "Oh, oh, Yahi. That feels so wonderful."

"I figured it did. It is a little known erogenous zone that women have." He continued to work the area.

"Ooh, ooh." She was so near.

Yahi quickly withdrew and dismounted.

She turned over. "What did you stop for? I was so close to coming."

He disposed of the condom. "That's why I stopped."

"You big tease. Get a girl all worked up and then you pull out."

He crawled back on the bed and kissed her to shut her up. "Hush. I am ready to feed my son now."

CHAPTER 23

*Y*ahi pulled the crotchless panties from her body and tossed them in the trash. He lubed up again so he wouldn't tear her as he entered. He looked down at Bethany. She was looking at him like she wanted to kill him. She was still pissed because he forced her orgasm away. "On your back, my princess. The vaginal probe is about to begin."

She parted her thighs but covered her private parts with her hands. "What is the password?"

"Very horny prince."

She removed one hand and used the other to part her lips. Her clitoris was dark pink and swollen. She was ready, even without the lube. "How bad do you want it, princess?"

"Don't make me beg, Yahi. I want you now." She moved her finger down and pushed it deep inside herself. "I'm going to do it myself if you don't hurry."

He removed her hand. "Wicked girl. There will be no masturbating in my presence unless that is my fantasy one night." He smiled. "And tomorrow night will be that night." He guided himself in.

Bethany held her legs open and then sat up to see him slide into her. "Come to me, Yahi." He moved in and kissed her. Her stomach wiggled just as he was about to withdraw.

"It moved."

Bethany nodded. "He's awake and ready for dinner."

He frowned. "No, I might hurt you."

"Don't be silly. He's protected in my womb."

Yahi moved back in cautiously and laid on her. Her belly moved against his. "Wow." He gushed. "There's life moving inside of you."

Bethany used her vaginal walls to suck him in. "Stop playing, Yahi and take me now."

He snapped back to reality and slid into her. Bethany clawed at his back. He flipped her over until she was seated on his lap facing him. He moved her up and down with his upper body muscles. Bethany bounced on him. Yahi strained. "I'm about to bust a nut." Bethany straddled him and he moved her back and forth like a glider. Bethany trembled. "Oh, I'm coming for sure this time." She came calling his name loud enough to wake everyone in the hotel.

Yahi saw stars when he exploded. "Marry me, Bethany or I will die without you."

Al-Shar did not take the announcement of her wedding nicely. "What is the meaning of this, Bethany?" he asked as he slid the society section of the newspaper toward her.

"It is a wedding announcement."

"Why did you agree to marry him?"

"Because he proposed."

"But you're carrying my child."

"Technically, I'm not really sure."

He scowled at her. "I figured that out a couple of days ago. His or mine, it really doesn't matter. I will love it anyway." He pounded his fist on the table. "You cannot marry him."

"I'm a grown woman, Al-Shar Khan. I can marry any one I want to."

"No, you can't sweet, Bethany. You can't marry Yahi because you're already married to me."

Her mouth opened and closed like a tuna. "Huh? What are your talking about?"

"Abdul married us."

"When?"

"Do you remember the belly-dancing incident?"

"No, only what you told me."

"Do you recall smoking the water pipe?"

"Yeah, way too much. I was wasted."

"Well, so was I, but Abdul and Khalaf decided that we needed to be married, so Abdul performed the ceremony while we were both semi-conscious."

"What?" she screamed. "I don't believe you."

He pulled the marriage license out of his pocket and handed it to her. It was her handwriting all right. She screamed again. "How long have you known?"

"A while."

"And you didn't tell me?"

"I was never going to tell you. I was going to have the marriage annulled when you returned to the United States. You were supposed to stay here a couple of weeks, but you didn't go home. I fell in love with you the moment I saw you in that bazaar and I just couldn't have the marriage annulled once I realized that we had slept together and consummated it. And now you're engaged to some blue-blooded, snot nosed prince who could possibly be the father of our child."

"Don't blame this on me. You should have told me. Then things might be different."

"Does he know about us?"

"Of course not."

"So, I'm your dirty little secret?"

"No, you are my lover."

"Put the marriage off for four more months."

"I can't marry him now anyway. That would make me a bigamist."

"So what are we going to do?"

"I'm going to tell him the truth. That this might not be his child. And he really wants this baby."

"So do I. And the mother. We can be so happy together."

∾

She had done some pretty low things in her life, but tailing a man was an all time low. She was tired of all this secrecy with Al-Shar. So she decided to follow him to see just what he did when he wasn't with her. Bethany had rented a car and waited for him to leave his house and then she followed him at a distance. Another car got in line in between their two cars and seemed to be following him too. She looked at the sign. He was headed for the Valley of the Kings. "Why is he going there at this time of night?"

The two cars stopped just outside of a nearby cemetery. Al-Shar got out and opened the trunk of his car. The car door of the other car opened and another man got out. Bethany squinted. It looked like Jamaal. He went to the back of his car and opened the trunk. Someone whistled and a woman appeared. Bethany's jealously level rose. Al-Shar took a bag out of the trunk and handed it to her. The woman kissed him and disappeared back into the cemetery. Several other women appeared and Jamaal and Al-Shar distributed more bags to them. The trunks closed and the two cars drove away.

"He was telling the truth," she said as she started up the car. "He has been telling the truth all this time. He's not a bandit. He really is feeding the poor." She headed back to the bungalow more confused now than ever. If he was out looting or killing, she could have gotten a quickie annulment from him. He was a humanitarian, a kind hearted man who thought about others. It should not have surprised her. He took care of her when she was sick, lovingly feeding her soup. Bethany grabbed her stomach. The nausea had returned. She was tired and she was probably overdoing it.

Mark started up the car and waited until Bethany's car passed him and then he followed the other two cars that headed in the opposite direct. One of them he knew belonged to Al-Shar Khan. So the bastard had survived the bullet and was out in the cemeteries delivering something to women. He didn't know or care about any of that. He was more interested in finding out the secret of the man behind the mask. He continued to drive behind the two cars as they headed for Cairo. A couple of hours later they stopped in front of the last place in the world he expected. The royal palace. Al-Shar stepped out of the car and removed his mask and beard, revealing his true identity.

"Well, I'll be damned."

"What do you want?' Al-Shar asked when he recognized the number on the caller ID. "I think we need to talk."

"You tried to kill me the last time that you just wanted to talk."

"But it's important. You can bring someone to search me this time. I have some information you might be interested in. It's about Prince Amasis."

"Why would information about him interest me?"

"Because I know that you've heard about his engagement to Ms. Dailet."

"So, what of it?"

"Do you know that she's pregnant?"

"Yes, old news."

"I know you love her."

"So."

"You're not making this easy. I have her and if you want her you have to meet me."

"What did you say?"

"I have taken Ms. Dailet hostage and if you want to see her again you better meet me."

"How do I know that you've telling the truth?"

"Listen to this. Say something Bethany."

"Al-Shar. Mark's telling the truth." He'd know that voice anywhere.

"I will kill you if you harm one hair on her head. Or harm that child. Where are you?"

"A place where it all began. King Amasis' tomb."

"I'm on my way." He hung up the phone and dialed the bungalow to tell George what was happening. Then he called Jamaal and filled him in. "I'm going to get her back."

"He's on his way, Bethany."

"I'm not surprised. That's how he is."

"Yes, he's an Egyptian action hero." Mark rubbed his jaw. "He's got some good moves. He nearly broke my jaw with a kick."

Mark had snatched her off the streets in broad daylight as she left her doctor's office. The pregnancy was progressing, but she didn't want to know the sex. She was old-fashioned like that. And then she went and got herself kidnapped again. *Maybe I'm cursed, she mused as she watched Mark pace. Maybe I should not have opened the doors to that tomb.*

"What if I told you that I know who Al-Shar really is?"

That caught her attention. "Who is he?"

"You're never going to believe it in a billion years."

"How did you find out?"

"I followed him just like you did the other night. Well, actually, I was following you, and then I just got caught up in the intrigue. I followed him after you left and that's when I found out his true identity." Mark looked out of the entrance of the cliff. "He's here."

"What are you going to do to him?"

"Your interest in a man who's been deceiving you overwhelms me. Is he that good in bed?"

"Yes, he's an excellent lover."

"And Prince Amasis?"

"He's pretty good too. Very imaginative."

"I can't picture you doing two men."

"That's because you don't know me as well as you think you do. Our relationships are very complicated."

"And you're pregnant."

She shrugged her shoulders. "Go figure."

"And which one is the father?"

"I haven't a clue."

Mark laughed. "You certainly are entertaining. But we could have been so happy together. I don't really like children, but I could have probably tolerated one."

Al Shar appeared in the entrance of the cliff. "Are you okay, Bethany?"

"She's fine. We were just having the loveliest conversation. I often wondered why a person wears a mask. Of course, it adds to the mystery, but my guess is that it's just to hide a secret. One the police would be interested in."

"I'm not afraid of the police. I haven't committed any crimes."

"They think you've been looting these tombs. Both you and this Jamaal fellow."

"I would never do such a thing. I love Egypt. It is part of me."

"I know that this is true. You have been doing everything in your power to stop the looting. Don't look so surprised. I have been doing my home-work." He kept the gun trained on Bethany. "And you're a humanitarian. You give food and clothing to the poor and provide them with shelter when you find it."

"Not a big secret either," Al replied. "The media has made me into a bandit though. I told Bethany all of this a long time ago."

"But I never believed it until recently."

Mark laughed. "Tell him what changed your mind?"

"I followed you the other night…to the cemetery in Luxor."

"What? You could have been killed. What if the police would have shown up?"

"Then we would have been in jail together."

"Not funny, Bethany. You're pregnant. You have to be careful."

"Yeah, like not letting myself get kidnapped for a second time."

Mark apologized. "Sorry about that. She was leaving the doctor's office. I couldn't help it."

"How's the baby?" Al-Shar asked.

"Strong and healthy."

"Good."

Mark interrupted them. "Please give me a break. I have a gun here. I'm trying to say something."

"Mark seems to think that he knows your true identity."

Al-Shar turned to Mark. "Do you?"

"Yes. I was following Bethany that night when she was following you. But instead of following her home I followed you home to Cairo."

"So I live in Cairo. I have homes all over the world."

"Really? And how can you afford that? I know how. I will keep it a secret for a price and free passage out of Egypt. I want a pardon from all crimes."

"I don't bargain with murderers." Al replied.

"Well, I'm not exactly a murderer. I didn't kill your father, Bethany. We got into an argument and he tried to attack me. He slipped and hit his head on a table."

"Why were you arguing?"

"He wouldn't back me in an investment because of what you told him about my shady business deals."

"I'm still not going to bargain with you," Al replied.

"I have a gun on the woman you love."

"He has a point," Bethany replied.

"Sure I do. Come with me Bethany and I will tell you who he really is."

"I already know who he is?"

Both men looked at her. "You do?" Al-Shar asked.

Bethany nodded. "You're Prince Amasis."

Al-Shar removed his mask and hood. "How did you find out?"

She pointed to his finger. "That ring. Only princes have it. And there were other things. The arm wound, the fact that you both wanted a houseful of children, other things only a woman would know."

"Are you terribly angry with me?"

"Oh, yeah," Bethany replied. "Your mother said you were wild. You're lucky that Mark's holding the gun and not me."

"At least the baby is legitimate."

"Not helping."

Mark cleared his throat. "I'm sorry for interrupting the two of you again, but I'm still holding the gun."

"She knows now, so what else have you got?"

"She knows, but Egypt doesn't. I bet I can make a lot of money off this story."

"Yahi, Yahi, Yahi. How many times have I told you that women are nothing but trouble?" Khalaf moved so fast that Mark never knew what hit him. The gun flew out his hands and he hit the ground unconscious.

"Khalaf," Bethany shouted. "What are you doing here?"

"I was just in the neighborhood, paying my respects to our dead pharaoh. You talked so much about the place I felt I really needed to see it. Imagine my surprise to hear that you were being held hostage again." He untied her while Yahi retrieved the gun.

"Mad moves," Yahi said giving Khalaf props from his sneak attack.

"I have my moments." He chuckled. "When I'm off the pipe."

Bethany grabbed Khalaf and hugged him. "Thanks."

"You're welcome. Yahi your woman is all over me." He kissed her on the forehead. "I couldn't let anything happen to my god-child."

"What?" Bethany asked as she released him.

Yahi shrugged his shoulders. "Just look at it this way. The child will have an interesting life. His father is my god-father and look how good I turned out."

Bethany burst into tears.

"Maybe that was a poor example," Khalaf replied.

"It's just hormones. In another four months, it will all be over." Yahi's cell phone rang. "It's father." He answered it. "Yes, sir. No, sir. I'm on my way." He put the phone away. "He wants to see all of us immediately."

"Are you disappointed in me, father?" Yahi asked after the police carted Mark away and they arrived at the palace. Unfortunately, bad news travels faster than a limousine."

"No," Waheed replied. "Not disappointed. Just confused. I thought I told you to give up your other personality before you got into trouble.

Yahi smiled innocently. "Bethany likes the mask."

"I do not," she said in her own defense.

The king looked down on her from his throne. "And look at you all pregnant and glowing. I thought you had more sense than Yahi and Jamaal. You could have gotten hurt."

"Sorry, Your Highness."

"Call, me Papa."

"Yes, Papa."

"I don't know what to do with you kids. My baby daughter has been married barely two months and already she is knocked up."

Jamaal lowered his head. "Sorry, father. It is all my fault."

"And you, Khalaf. Honestly. Getting your father to perform a wedding ceremony while Yahi and Bethany are stoned. You shouldn't give a female a water pipe. Bad future king."

Khalaf shrugged his shoulders. "I am my father's son."

The king tried not to laugh. "Of course you are." He turned back to

Bethany. "Now you, young lady." He shook his head. "Romancing it up with two men at the same time. This has got to stop. You will be queen one day."

"Yes, Papa, but in my own defense, it was Yahi who tricked me. He's kind of hard to resist if you know what I mean?"

"Yes, he is my son. I know exactly what you mean. And I just want to say that your breasts are phenomenal. My grandchild will be wed fed."

Bethany blushed. The Amasis men had no shame. "Yes, Papa. Both babies to be exact."

"Yes, Kasia will be getting pretty big too. She has her mother's breasts."

"No, I don't mean her. Yahi and I are having twins." Yahi looked over at her and promptly fainted. Bethany looked down at him and smirked triumphantly. "I can keep a secret too."

"Wake your brother-in-law up, Jamaal," the king ordered. "This palace is getting crazier by the minute."

"Two babies," Yahi said when he came to. "What are we going to do with two babies?"

"Al-Shar can raise the other one," Bethany replied sarcastically.

"That's still me. It's my real name, actually. Yahi Al-Shar Ahmose Amasis." He paced. "I have a lot of plans to make, cradles to order and I have to hire a wet nurse."

"I plan to breast feed my own babies."

"Uh Uh," Yahi uttered. "Those are my breasts." He hurried out of the throne room.

"You are going to have to have him committed before this is over," Bethany whispered to her father-in-law.

"I know. Wait until his mother and his god-parents find out. There is going to be pandemonium."

"I have to leave," Khalaf said. "I have a wedding to plan."

"Whose?" Bethany asked.

"Yours and Yahi."

"But we're already married."

"Yes, but a different one this time with friends and family present and the two of you sober."

"Spare no expense," the king told him. "But make it quick. We don't have much time before the stork arrives." He clapped his hands together. "This has been a blessed year. My beautiful wife and I will celebrate our fortieth wedding anniversary soon. We've found the remains of our beloved ancestors, two of my children are married, and will be moving out of my palace, and I'm going to be blessed with three grandchildren. What more can a king want?"

Bethany looked up. *You hear that Father? I did good.*

THE END

THANK YOU FOR READING

Did you enjoy this book?

We invite you to leave a review at your favorite review site(s), such as Goodreads, Amazon, Barnes & Noble, etc.

DID YOU KNOW THAT LEAVING A REVIEW...

- Helps other readers find books they may enjoy.
- Gives you a chance to let your voice be heard.
- Gives authors recognition for their hard work.
- Doesn't have to be long. A sentence or two about why you liked the book will do.

~

Don't miss out on your next favorite book!

~

Join the Melange Books mailing list at
www.melange-books.com/mail.html

Subscriber Perks Include:

- First peeks at upcoming releases.
- Exclusive giveaways.
- News of book sales and freebies right in your inbox.
- And more!

ABOUT THE AUTHOR

Imari Jade hails from Marrero, Louisiana, where she works as a financial analyst. She collects anime and Asian drama and considers herself a multi-genre author. She is the mother of three sons and does the bulk of her writing riding on a bus to and from work five days a week. Currently she writes for Siren-Bookstrand, Passion in Print, Melange Books, Phaze Books, Caliburn Press, and Totally Bound.

~

Eager to hear what's next for Imari Jade?

Join her mailing list at
www.imarijade.com

~

Find Imari Jade Online
www.imarijade.com

Twitter
@imarijade

Facebook
www.facebook.com/Imari-Jades-Fan-Page-110285572341938/

ALSO BY IMARI JADE

FROM MELANGE BOOKS

Novels

In Love With a Dark Stranger

Novellas

Skinship

Featured in the following Anthologies

Forbidden Fruit

Having My Baby

Midnight Thirsts